Blessing to you, sister.
Fredrick Hull

THE UNKNOWN
PROPHET

The Divine Calling

BY
FREDRICK W. HULL
COPYRIGHT 2019

1

Printed In The United States

The Unknown Prophet: The Divine Call

Printed by KP

Book Design: Oliviaprodesign

DEDICATION

First, I am so thankful and humbled that the very Creator of Heaven and Earth would use me to write my 3rd book. I am still amazed that His Grace has covered me; and inspired me to write Christian Fictions.

Even though I still struggle with the English language, my mind is still boggled that He would lead me down this certain pathway to write books for His Kingdom. Stories with lessons on how The Kingdom of God works in people's lives, and the dark forces of Satan's kingdom that comes against them.

I still love to teach the Scripture's from a Hebrew understanding and their culture. To see people's lives changed for His Glory. I have been given a ministry mandate of restoring the heart of man back to the heart of their Father and God.

Secondly, once again, a deep apperception for my wife for standing with me through the last five years of health issues, also encouraging me to write on subjects that can give the Body of Messiah a different perspective on certain issues that they are challenged with. With so much false teachings and a different Gospel that has crept into the American Churches. It is His Kingdom that we need to know and understand what His Spirit is trying to teach us to be truly blessed and obedient to His Scriptures. By this book and my other two books that were written in the last three years.

They are; Divorce from Satan a story of a young man who was greatly deceived by Satan. Then Noah's Journal Of The Last Days where Noah wrote his own journal of what his days were like until his death.

You can order these books through Barnes & Noble, Mardel stores, Amazon.com and KDP. Be sure to do a book review on Amazon.com for me and tell others about my books.

Shalom and Blessings to you and your family.

Table of Contents

INTRODUCTION

Most Christians are not aware of several Prophesies that were given many years ago and today about the Native Americans rising again and taking their rightful place in the Kingdom of Elohim (God).

Many believe, as myself, that some of the Tribes of Indians are a part of the Lost Tribes of Israel. The Cherokee nation at one time taught their people back in early parts of their existence up to the early 1800's. For they had taught their people that they came from Tribe of Gad. (10 lost tribes). They even had a Holy book that was later discovered to be identical to the First Five Books of the Old Covenant (OT) by a local missionary that had lived with them for a period of time.

They knew the Great Spirit in the Sky (**YeHehaWaH**eha He who creates) and His Son that He sent to the Earth to bring mankind back to their Creator. (**YoHeWah**si-known as Jesus). Sadly, many Native Americans has been subdued by Satan's kingdom over the last 500 years. It was a great deception he placed in their spiritual culture as a people of great faith and integrity for this region they called home. Contrary to the white man religion that came across the big pond and started to dominate this new land for them. The US government propaganda began to paint these native Americans as savages, ignorant and barbaric and great sinners who opposes their faith and Church beliefs. Thus, the great deception began to get rid of these savages and to genocide them as a race of people. Either they converted to the white man lifestyle and religion or be put to death.

At one time, in this new country, there were 500 different tribes of Native Americans. Over the years of civil war amongst themselves, the beginning of this new race that brought plagues and disease that would even wipe out a whole tribe. Sadly, by the 1700's and 1800's this number fell tremendously. The one's left were fighting to stay alive by seeking peace with the people that became their new taskmasters. Still they trusted **YeHehaWaH**eha (He who Creates) and their spirits and pride were never broken. So, therefore I felt inspired to write a fictional story about one of the most important offices in the Five-Fold Ministry that Paul tells us in Ephesians 4 that the office of a Prophet that Elohim (God) has used since the time of Moses. It is too bad that this office has had a lot of self-proclaiming Prophets, who have done a great injustice among His people. The Scriptures give us great insight about this office and its proper function for the Body of Messiah.

This is the way our Father Elohim meant this office to be in the OT and NT. After divorcing Israel and causing Judah to fall, that in The Last Days He will have reunited them both back as One Nation. So, sit back and enjoy a story that sounds so familiar to us throughout the OT stories. And watch the Spirit of the Prophet deal with the dark forces of Satan's kingdom and wanting to bring Elohim (God) people back to him in a divine relationship. Oh, how we desperately need the True Prophets of Elohim (God) to help rightfully govern His Church and reach those who have had gone astray from their loving Father and Creator.

It is Time to come home prodigal sons and daughters, for when you see the Temple in Jerusalem being rebuilt, time is short, and Satan and his evil forces will wreak havoc upon this earth like never before. Throughout the many centuries of humans, man has always sought to go further and find new lands that they can dominate and rule with power and might. Whoever was the strongest had been embedded with that very spiritual seed of rebellion and conquest.

They wanted to be worshiped as a god or those spirits that seem to rule their very atmosphere of humans. In which these spirits have greatly persuaded man away from the worshiping of their true Creator and Elohim (God). The battle for humans' spirit and souls began when man was kicked out of a garden of paradise and where true peace reigned and ruled. The Creator had over centuries try to inter-vein with man by his Holy Angels with a message of hope and love and peace.

Finally, the Creator sent His Son to die for mankind and take on the great judgment of Sin that had engulfed the whole planet of Earth. This message was received with great hope that finally man was able to have a Father and Son relationship with their Creator and Elohim (God). Yet this message of hope and love was soon overcome by the darkness of sin and those who ruled the very air that men breathe. It almost seemed that this dark force was winning, but there was always a remnant of true believers that would stay faithful to their Creator no matter what man or spirits that controlled them like puppets. This message of Righteousness dug its heels deep to those who served their Creator with all they had to offer.

This message of hope and love would soon be tainted with man's own doctrines and beliefs. It began to cause a religion to take over lands and man for their kingdom and not the true Kingdom of Elohim (God). This white man's religion became so large and powerful that it began its conquest over man's souls and spirits with a law of legalism. This religion seemed to bind up man more than the spirit of sin that came upon man when he or she were born on this earth.

This man's religion dug its claws into a society; and if a man or town did not receive it, the outcome was deadly to its harmless victims. This religion system dominated everywhere its follower went to conquer and make man submit to their beliefs.

But somewhere in the vast population of humans the old ways of the instruction of Elohim (God) were passed down from generation to generation, hoping to spark a light into the very darkness of mankind's hearts. Many years before this false-religion came to this country where no white man had made his mark upon; even though over the centuries many had made their way to explore and wonder at the vastness of this country.

Its beauty and landscape that made many believe that this frontier was the new promised land. The natives knew that this was their home and felt safe for many centuries.

In the mid 1500's natives began to see strange ships come to their land that had traveled across the big pond. Their curiosity got the best of them when a white man came with goods to trade for food and furs. At first, it seemed these white men came in peace and to live in harmony with the natives. These white men had long sticks that made a loud sound when he lit the fuse and pulled the trigger. The natives knew then that their weapons were inferior to this long stick. Many of the natives were glad to trade with the white man but many felt uneasy and afraid that one day, their lives would be in great danger. As time went on, more white men came on their shores and their numbers began to grow and outnumber the natives. For the white men began to build great lodges and big communities and it seem there was no stopping them. Eventually the natives were forced from their homes on the shore lines and moved back into the interior of the land.

Many of the natives in this new frontier made treaties with the Red Coats (Great Britain) because promises were made for many supplies and even firearms and to be able to keep their land. Only if they joined them to fight against the white settlers that had committed treason against their country and King George II.

For the Red Coats had told them that they were not interested in this new frontier but to keep these settlers loyal to King George II and any other countries that would try to invade their land. Soon the natives would realize that they were lied too and used as puppets for King George II. They were eventually forced off their lands and moved to the south and eventually the land west of the Mississippi River. IT IS TIME TO KNOW THE GREAT **YeHehaWatteha** (I AM YOUR FATHER) and the True Messiah, YoHeWah-si (Jesus) His Son.

Chapter 1

The Visitation

It was in the late winter of 1780, a small village that was called Chota located in the eastern slopes part of Appalachian Mt. of Tennessee. There was a middle-aged Cherokee woman named Morning Star, who ancestors had taught that their family was from a lost tribe that was far away across the Big Pond. Their ancestors had travel over the years to come to this place that was their New Promised Land. It was through the certain women who were chosen to breed a son to keep their divine heritage and blood line alive and to follow the ways of their True Creator (**YaHehaWatteHa**) and His Laws for mankind.

She had been married almost 25 years to a Chief Elder (Spotted Wolf) who was next in line for the Head Elder-ship of the whole Cherokee nation. For years they had been trying to have a son who came from the Wolf Clan. It was this Clan that raised up Elders of the Cherokees and warriors.

There were 6 other clans that made up the governmental structure of the United Keetoowah Band of Cherokees. Each village was made of a certain clan that has its function within the main village where the Chief Elder lived. The village of Chota was the Wolf Clan camp where warriors and Chiefs were born, trained and raised to take their rightful place within the government of the Cherokee Tribe.

The other clans included the Wild Potato (farmers & harvesters) Clan, then there was Clan of the Long Hairs (teachers & keepers of the Law), the Deer Clan (hunters & and tanners & foot messengers). Then the Red Tail Clan (keepers of birds), the Blue Holly Clan (keepers of children & growing gardens). Finally, the 7th member were called the Paint Clan where the Shamans (were Holy medicine men) born and trained for their priestly ministry over the tribes.

Each camp had a designated Elder and a Medicine Man to lead their clan in the ways of the Keetoowah Cherokees. The Cherokees were well known among other tribes to be the best organizes and one of the largest tribes in land they called New The Promise Land.

Yet, they still had other tribes that hated and feared them for their great size in population (10,000) and enormous land.

These camps were spread out over miles in all directions. Morning Dove had always tried to stay true to her beliefs even when the Shaman would commit treason to their Great Creator and turn to the dark spirits that would disguise themselves as great warriors of the past.

Slowly over the years their influence had made their way into all the camps of all the Natives that lived in their own regions of the land. Morning Dove knew that her Creator would not let her down and that one day she would have her promised son and that he would help keep the ways of their Creator. It was later that night, as she began to fall asleep, that her spirit seemed restless and that she could not get settled at all.

Her husband Spotted Wolf turned over and gave her a kiss and told her not to worry about anything. Morning Star gave a sigh and knew that she needed to sleep and then turned over. As she closed her eyes, suddenly she found herself walking down this path that seemed long and dark.

There was a light fog covering the pathway she found herself on. At first, she could not understand what was happening. Yet in her spirit she felt it was okay. She then noticed that there were no birds flying not even the noises of the animals that roamed their woods. Her heart began to fear and suddenly this great big warrior like man appeared by her and she fell to her knees and began to think he was there to kill her. The warrior took her hand and told her that he was the angel that she met as a young girl and not to fear him. Suddenly her mind replayed that moment when she was very young and was at her prayer place and while praying to her Holy Creator. It was then when she learned about the Creator sending His Son to die for her sins.

She never forgot the anointing that came upon her when she accepted the Creators Son **YoHeWaHsi** (Jesus) as her Lord and Savior. The angel bent over and raised her up and told her that she needed not to fear him and not to bow down to him. only **YoHeWaHsi** was worthy of this act of worship. He began to walk down the pathway holding her hand. He wanted to reveal what was going to happen very soon to her.

She began to feel the same warm peace that had touch her back in her childhood.

She could not remember his name and stopped to ask him what his name was? He looked into her brown eyes and told her that his name is Gabriel, a Holy Messenger for the Holy Creator. The angel stopped and turned to look at her and said that he would explain later what was happening to her and not be fearful. As she was getting ready to answer him, he suddenly disappeared from her sight.

She found herself all alone and began to look around to see that this world was not like her world, but it was like this world was and so vivid, everything was so transparent. Then she heard a voice tell her to keep walking down this pathway and not to fear for what she would experience and see with her own eyes. She kept walking down the pathway and noticed that a cloud of darkness was swarming around like black birds and descending to the pathway she was walking. Suddenly the vivid colors of the trees and grass became like the color of the ashes of an old campfire. As she kept walking down the pathway trying to find where it was leading.

She came to a hill and she became horrified to see a valley of dead bones that went for miles. She became so startled to see that these bones had native clothes on them and some of them still had their skins on the bones. She saw woman and children, the elderly and even warriors piled up as if they have been slaughtered by a great enemy. Her heart began to break, and she wondered why all these fellow natives were dead. Then the tears began to flow out of her eyes, she could not contain them, and she fell down on her knees. She just wept and cried out to the angel and asked why she was seeing this valley of dead bones. It seemed it was for eternity to her while she was lying face down while her heart was broken.

Then she felt this gentle hand on her shoulder and heard this voice tell her to rise. As she got up and looked, it was Gabriel standing by her reaching out to hold her hand and telling her to look toward the east. She felt that peace again as she did with her first encounter with this angel. Her tears were gone and that hopeless was gone from her heart. She asked why she was looking towards the east and he just pointed his finger that way and said to watch what was going to happen next. The scenery changed in front of her and she saw her village up close.

Then she heard a baby crying and saw her husband coming out of their hut holding a new born baby in his hands. Then Gabriel and she were standing in front of her hut and he told her that what she had just experienced was the spirit realm. That he was sent to her with 2 messages of what was going to happen to her soon.

Gabriel took her by the hands and told her that her Creator has heard her tears over the years of wanting to have a son and to honor her husband. She began to cry and started to rejoice with gladness. Then Gabriel told her that it would be not too long until she would become pregnant with her son. She began to think for a minute and turned to him and asked why did he show her that massive graveyard of her fellow natives?

He told her that he was sent to warn her that not too long after her son is born, a very dark force of evil would try destroy the natives. That the evil spirits would use the pale faces to carry their plan out with a disease that will almost wipe out half her nation and completely wipe entire tribes off the face of the earth.

She did not understand what he meant so she asked him what evil spirits he was talking about. He then told her to close her eyes and then open them up again. At first, she was hesitating, but she knew from the teaching of their holy man; Raven that there were good and evil spirits among all the natives that lived on this land.

So, she closed her eyes and opened them again and was shocked in what she saw. The very atmosphere where she stood seemed like her home, but she knew it was not the same as hers. The trees and the grass and the mountains had the same look except they were gloomy looking, and the air had a certain darkness that overshadowed the whole land. She turned and looked at Gabriel and noticed he had this shining light about him that even caused the darkness to flee from him.

He was dressed in clothing that was not recognizable to her and he stood about 9ft tall. She rubbed both of her eyes to make sure what she saw was real. Then he pointed towards her camp and she saw warrior like spirits walking among the people there.

Then Gabriel told her to watch what would happen next. He spoke with authority and told the warrior spirits to show themselves as they truly were. Suddenly in front of her they became like shift-changers which was common among many tribes in this region. She watched as they changed their forms from Indian like into a creature like form. Their hair was the purest black, their eyes were like serpents that were not like any other animals on the earth. She even noticed that their hands were like an old aged Indian except they were hairy and long. Even the smell that permeated from their flesh was like the Sulphur smell that only came from the deep caverns in the earth.

Morning Dove could not believe her eyes in what she just witnessed of these warrior-like spirits. Soon she realized that her people and even the holy men were greatly deceived that these warrior-like spirits were good spirits, yet they were demonic in their true nature. Gabriel then told her that this evil disease that was coming would come across the great pond with the white man as the carrier. They would deliberately place this disease on blankets that would be given to the tribes.

Thus, causing great devastation among the tribes and even the white men. For this is what she saw in her vision earlier. Morning Dove could not really understand the concept of this disease and then told Gabriel that the holy men had special herbs and prayers that would drive this disease away from them. He then grabbed her hands and told her even their holy herbs or even the holy men could not drive this evil force away from them.

She told him that many of her people trusted the white man and that they have done nothing against their tribe. Gabriel began to tell her that all pace faces are not alike, but there were more of them that wanted to get rid of the Native Americans and take their land from them. They wanted their lands with all its riches and minerals that would cause the white man to do anything for it. Plus, this evil disease would leave many with horrible scars and that many will take their own lives instead of living with this disease. She then asked him what she was supposed do about this? He said that there was nothing she could do but trust her Creator that her family would not be touched by any of this disease. Gabriel then smiled and told her that her promised child would live and grow up to be a holy prophet unto his people and others that would follow the message of righteousness and hope in their Great Creator. Morning Dove suddenly found herself all alone in front of her hut and knowing she must be prepared for that day of great joy having a son and also the coming evil force that would kill too many Indians and wipe out an entire tribe that would no longer exist. Later she learned that even Raven the holy man had a vision from the great spirit that he was bringing great judgment against the white man and a great warrior would lead them to victory over them.

Now came the hard part for her of waiting to get pregnant with a son that would bring glory to the Creator and her husband. Then about six months went by after she had received the Holy visit from Gabriel. She finally became pregnant after 25 years of being barren. It was spring time when nature started to become alive for all to see its beauty. Finally, Morning Dove's dream became a reality to her and her husband and their entire camp. Her Great Creator has answered her prayers and finally she felt complete as a woman and a wife.

After Spotted Wolf had come back from a Elder meeting where the Chief of the

Cherokee Nation lived. She couldn't wait to tell him the great news that she was with child. As he entered their hut, she threw herself into his arms and gave him a kiss that took him back for moment. She had this huge smile on her face, and he began to wonder why was she go excited to see him?

She told him to sit down and that she needed to tell him some great news. So, he sat down by her as she explained to him that he was finally going to have a son. Spotted Wolf jumped to his feet and let out the loudest war cry he had ever made in his life. The whole camp could hear him and many of them came running towards their hut to see what the commotion was all about. He then ran around the hut yelling he was going to be a father for the first time. Little did he know that Gabriel was standing by their hut, just smiling and raising his hands towards Heaven and giving thanks to the Holy One for this great occasion. Then Gabriel folded his arms and smiled and nodded his head and disappeared out of sight.

Chapter 2

A Son Is Given

It was early in the morning in the late fall of 1781, one could see the morning dew gleaming from the grass as the sun peaked over the hill side. All was quite in the village of Chota in the eastern slopes of the Appalachian Mt. of Tennessee. The birds began to sing that a new day had begun and there were some deer drinking from the Tellico River, being cautious of any danger to them.

The village of Chota was one of the largest among the Tsalagi Clan which belonged to the United Keetoowah Band of Cherokees. The Wolf Clan had encamped by the Tellico River; while the other six clans were spread out within a day or two of travel. The Chota village was where the Chief Elders were born along with warriors who oversaw of keeping their nation safe. There was a hut where Spotted Wolf was seen walking back and forth waiting for his son to come into the world. Inside the mid-wives were trying to comfort Morning Dove in her birth pains and trying to keep her in a squatting position so that the promised child would make its much-anticipated entrance into the world. The nearby huts could hear her screaming from the great pain and knowing her age was late and had caused concerns among them for her being late in age for childbirth. Raven the medicine man was making his chants and blowing his holy smoke around the hut. Inside Morning Dove was trying to show her courage to the mid-wives that she was able handle the birth of her son.

As Raven made his way in the hut to bless the coming child, Morning Dove suddenly had her eyes opened and saw four demon like spirits following the medicine man. Under her breath, she prayed with her prayer language and asking the Great Spirit to protect her son. Meanwhile the mid-wives thought she was losing her mind praying in a language that was not their native tongue. They thought this child birth was too much for her and they asked Raven to come closer and to chant and blow the holy smoke over her. As he approached her, he began to shake violently as the four demons kept telling him to pray harder. Finally, the promised child came forth into a world of fresh crisp air that caused him to cry aloud for the first time. Morning Dove was so relieved that her son was finally here. She motioned the mid-wives to hand her new son to her and she held him close to her chest. Suddenly she could hear Spotted Wolf give a loud war cry that his son had arrived and started to dance with great joy. It seemed the whole camp was celebrating with him his son's birth.

Little did they know that an angel from Heaven stood outside the hut and was raising his hands towards Heaven giving thanks to the Great Creator. Then Raven began to blow his holy smoke upon the child, the ritual of blessing every child born in this camp. In his mind this was the promised warrior that would grow up and finally get rid of the white men who came upon their land.

As he blew the smoke, he was taken back that the smoke could not touch the child but rather it came back to him. Raven was startled at this and thought he would try it again. He took in a deep breath from his ceremonial pipe and blew harder this time. Once again, the smoke came back into face and caused him to stumble back and cough.

This time he became outraged as the demons clawed their hands into his soul causing him to scream aloud. Morning Dove knew what was happening and told him and the mid-wives to leave and let her husband come in to see his son. Spotted Wolf was shaking his head as he came in and wondered why Raven was so mad! But his concern soon vanished, as he began to hold his first born for the first time.

The child had his eyes and nose and black hair that glistened from the campfire. Except he noticed that his son had a gray streak on his right side of his hair. He was so overwhelmed that he began to hold the child upwards and gave thanks to the Great Spirit. Morning Dove began to cry at seeing her husband hold their son as a very proud father. She too noticed the gray streak in his hair and thought this was a great sign from her Creator. As Spotted Wolf finished his prayer unto the Great Creator, he could hear Raven throwing a fit about what had happened earlier. For the whole camp could hear his screaming and lamenting over what just happened in the hut. They were all unaware that the four demons were poking him and yelling at him for what happened in the hut with the child. Raven could not understand why this happened to him and he promised them that it wouldn't happen again. He kept telling himself that his potion needed more ingredients to be more powerful for the next time. The demons kept telling him that this was the promised warrior that was going get rid of the white man and drive them back across the big pond. Meanwhile, back at the hut, Spotted Wolf told his wife in the days to come of presenting their son in the holy ceremony of dedication; then they will give a proper name for him.

Morning Dove just smiled and agreed they would give their son his proper name that would symbolize his character and life to the Cherokee people. As Spotted Wolf left his hut, he heard a commotion, going by the water jugs on the side of his hut. He noticed a brown looking fox who had a gray streak on him. He was amazed to see this kind of fox around his hut and that must be sign from the Creator on this day of birth of his son. For in his culture a brown fox was normal and yet it was rare with a gray streak on its side. He knew then that must be a good omen from the mighty warriors of the past.

He knew then what he should name his son at the ceremonial dedication. He then made his way to visit Raven and see what all the commotion was earlier. Morning Dove was tired and wrapped her son with beaver felt and cuddled her son next to her to get some much-needed rest. As she fell asleep, she found herself waking down this pathway that she had walked many times before. As she came to this certain crossing on the pathway, she stood in the middle of it.

As she stood there for a moment, she could hear a voice of a bear coming down the other pathway. As it got closer, she knew it was Scar-Face the black bear that has caused such great havoc among the local tribes. For many believe that this was a spirit of a warrior that been killed by his own tribe and that he was out for revenge for his death.

As the bear got closer to her, she suddenly felt no fear but peace for some reason. She just knew the bear was going to kill her right there on the spot. Suddenly she heard a noise from the other path and saw a gray like fox charging the bear. Morning Dove knew that foxes were a lot faster than a bear more cunning than any other animal. The bear stood on his back legs and made a loud roar against the gray fox. Then the fox ran circles around the bear so fast that it made the bear stumble and bow down before Morning Dove. She was very shocked to see this happening to her, not believing what had just happened. Suddenly Scar-Face stood up and ran the opposite of way from Morning Dove.

 The small gray fox was just sitting in front of her when she felt that somebody was standing behind her. She turned around and saw Gabriel standing there with a smile on his face. Now she knew why Scar-Face left so quickly from seeing the Holy Messenger of the Great Creator.

She was so relieved that he was there and wondered why he showed up at this time. He told her that he had come to her to give her new-born son his name. She askcd what his name and the meaning of his birth into their family would be. He told her that his name would be Gray Fox and that he would become a prophet unto his people and bring great wisdom and understanding of who they were in the Creators Kingdom. Morning Dove just stood there and was thankful that the Great Creator would allow her to see these visions and promises about her son. Then the gray fox and Gabriel turn around and disappeared from her sight. Suddenly she found herself lying beside her son and just smiled with great joy that her son finally was born for a great purpose in life. She finally fell asleep knowing her job was to train her son to become a mighty prophet unto her people and those who aligned with the nation of the Cherokees.

Tomorrow would be a new day and she could not wait to see her son grow up with a holy purpose and destiny. Plus, she knew that her husband would be pleased with the name for their son. The next day came and the preparations for their son's dedication had to be planned and the invitation for all Cherokees to come and see their son being dedicated to the great and holy Creator. For the news had traveled fast throughout the entire Cherokee clans that Spotted Wolf and Morning Dove were finally blessed with a son. This was a great joyful time among all them and to come and see this great wonder of a child being born unto a woman that was past her time to have a child.

Later that day, Morning Dove needed rest from yesterday's great event and went to lay down in her hut. As she snuggled up against her son, a bright light lit up the whole hut and cause her to get under her cover. She heard a voice saying to her; "Peace unto you Morning Dove". She then knew it was Gabriel the angel who had come before with the great news of her having a son. As she took the cover off, she saw him kneeling before her and her child. He had this big grin on his face as if he had done this before. He then asked her if she was pleased with her son? She began to cry and tell him that this was the greatest gift she could ask for in life. He then stretched out his hands and asked if could hold the young child?

She picked up the child and handed him over to the angel and watched as he stood on his feet and raised the child towards heaven. Gabriel gave praise and thanks to the Creator and began to bless the child in a beautiful language that only comes from Heaven. The room soon was filled with this white cloud and the very presence of something Holy that was not human. Morning Dove found herself on her face and worshiping her Holy Creator with her prayer language.

It seemed to her that this lasted a long time and she did not want this Holy Cloud to go from her. Soon she was able to get off the ground and to see Gabriel handing her child back to her. He then told her that the blood of her Messiah was upon him, to protect him from any harm and that the enemy would try to take his life. Then out of nowhere another angel appeared by him and this angel was dressed in a full amour like a warrior going into battle.

Gabriel told her that this was Michael the Arch-Angel, the leader of warrior angels who protects the Creators creations and His people from the evil one and his demons. Michael reached out his hand to her and told her that it would be a great honor to protect this child who was ordained by the Creator to bring the message of righteousness to her people and other tribes. His hands seemed so gentle compared to his rugged look as a mighty warrior. She noticed his hair was just gleaming with a golden look to it and his appearance was like nothing she had seen before meeting Gabriel. Suddenly the glow that was on the angel came upon the child and made his face to shine just like the angels.

Morning Dove was so overwhelmed by his voice and glowing so bright that she was wondered if people outside the hut could see the bright light. He reassured her that nobody could hear or see the glory shinning about the lodge. Then Michael knew instantly that there were demons just standing outside the lodge but could not enter it. One of the demons tried to get closer and look, but the glory from Michael and the baby caused the demon to fall back on his face. The other three knew then what was happening and grabbed the fourth and took off towards Raven's hut.

Michael and Gabriel both just laughed and then handed the baby back to Morning Dove and told her that Raven and his cohorts would try to harm her child but not worry because Michael would make sure that nothing happened to him in his lifetime. Meanwhile the 4 demons were trying to get their eye sight back from seeing the Glory upon the child. So, they went to Raven's hut that there was a certain reason his holy smoke would not touch the child earlier. Raven became so enraged about the news that he screamed out a very loud war cry. The whole camp heard him and just knew that he was upset with his making of potions and herbs. He just knew that this so-called bad spirit had make it tough for him to anoint the child and prepare him to become the savior of the Cherokee nation from the white man.

Back at Morning Dove hut, Michael the angel told her that he would keep his eyes upon her child until his job was done here on earth. They both wished her peace and vanished from her sight. She looked down upon her son and just knew he was headed for a great life and was proud of him already. It was getting late and it was time to lay down with him and feed him her milk. At that time Spotted Wolf came in for the night and told his two warriors to stand guard over their hut till morning. The whole camp all got settled in for the night and in the distance a family of wolves were crying out to the moon which was very bright.

It seemed that the woods were coming to life as the night creatures began to hunt for food. Raven was still fuming over what happened that day and was trying to figure out how to get this child anointed with the holy smoke at his dedication ceremony. He put on his prayer paint on and began to moan and chant for the spirits to come and give him the wisdom of overcoming the bad spirit that he thought was on the child. Then he went into a trance and began to shake violently as he prayed to the great spirit for wisdom.

The 4 demons were rubbing their crooked fingers together and wondering how they could make Raven do their beckoning and kill the child. They began to put their claws into his brain and soul and cause him to roll back his eyes and began to crawl on his stomach like a snake. This lasted for over an hour and finally Raven composed himself and just knew that he would have the victory over this child. Then he would help him to become a great warrior for the Cherokee nation. Even though his body was drenched from severe sweating, he now could go bed and sleep knowing the victory was his. The four demons just sat back and laughed amongst themselves at what a fool Raven was. How they had deceived him that was he was in control of them. Thinking they were good spirits of warrior's past. Raven knew that his work was cut out for him and he needed to spend more time his sweat hut to get wisdom from the spirits.

He had never had to deal with this kind of problem before and he was baffled at what happened to him at the ceremony. He closed his eyes as he was chanting more to the spirits for guidance on this most holy mission. By this time Spotted Wolf gave his wife and son a good night kiss and made sure their fire burned for a long time. The big day was coming tomorrow for this family that would change theirs lives forever. The countdown was on for Spotted Wolf.

Chapter 3

The Dedication Ceremony

It had been eight days since Morning Dove had given birth to her son and today was a day of great celebration among their camp and other camps who were invited for this joyful occasion. It seemed that hundreds of Cherokees came for the celebration and dedication of Spotted Wolf and Morning Dove's new born son.

Everyone came and stood outside their hut to watch the dedication of this special child. For some they believed Raven's report that this child was destined to become the great warrior that would help them to drive the white man back across the big pond. Many were just so happy that Morning Dove finally had a child after being barren for so long.

Unknown to the Indians, there were also another group of beings hiding behind the tree line to watch this human event take place. Even though they looked like Indians of the past life, they were demons that were assigned to each camp. On the north side of the camp there was another group of warriors that was shining like the sun, yet these were heavenly angel sent to watch this event take place and make sure their arch-enemies were not going to cause problems at the event. Spotted Wolf and Morning Dove were inside their hut holding their child. They looked at each other at the same time and asked what would be their son name? They both laughed and he told her go ahead and give the name she thought best for their son. She began to tell him about the vision she had right after he was born. She described the pathway and walking down it and running into Scar Face the old black bear.

Then how this gray fox came and ran around the bear so fast that he fell before her like he was worshiping her. Spotted Wolf began to laugh and told her how that day the child was born, and he left the hut and saw a gray fox drinking out of the water basin. He knew then that was a sign from the Great Spirit and that Gray Fox would be his sons name. They began to worship the Great Creator for these signs given to them and that this would be the name of their son. It was time for them to take their son out to be dedicated and let the Cherokee nation see their firstborn with name Gray Fox.

As they began to walk out of the hut, Morning Dove felt the urge to pray under her breath and just trust that all would be well today. As they stepped out of the hut, the whole camp let out a cry of celebration that could be heard miles away. The northern winds were brisk and cold as they made their way to the main camp fire. Morning Dove made sure her son was wrapped well with the fur of a fox as the snow began to come down slowly.

They both approached Raven as he was standing by the fire and was ready to perform the child's dedication as he had done for many years as the holy medicine man. The parents approached him and handed Gray Fox over to Raven. The child began to cry as he lifted him up towards the sky and to ask the Great Spirit to bless this child.

The child began to cry harder and harder as if something was wrong with him. Raven just laughed and told the crowd that this was the effect he had on all children that he has blessed. Everyone began to laugh and let out a cry. Morning Dove knew what was happening to her son because of the bad spirits that controlled Raven's life as the medicine man.

Raven spoke a few words over the parents and then began proclaiming that this was the child he saw in a vision a few years ago. That his child would grow up to be a mighty warrior among the Cherokees and help drive the white man off their land and back across the big pond. Many warriors there began to give a war cry out and started to dance as if they were going to war.

This news to Spotted Wolf was great to hear that his son was destined to become a great warrior. He really did not have a problem with the white man since he had seen a few white men over the past few years. They were mostly fur traders and traded white man gadgets that were helpful to his people. Finally Spotted Wolf raised his hands as if he was telling them to be quiet.

They all stopped, and he told Raven to go on with the ceremony because it was getting too cold for the baby. Raven then took his holy pipe and began to anoint Gray Fox as the true warrior for the Cherokee nation. He blew the smoke upon the baby and once again it would not touch him. Morning Dove just snickered under her breath and knowing here we go again with Raven. So, he tried again, and the smoke came back on his face and caused him to stumble back. He then screamed loudly and began to curse the bad spirit that was protecting this baby. The four demons showed up behind Raven and began told him that this was not a bad spirit of an Indian but an angel from the Great Spirit. Then one of the demons opened Raven eyes to see a glowing light about the baby. He had never seen this before in his life. This made him furious that his magic could not affect the baby.

Spotted Wolf grabbed his son and told Raven this was enough and it's time for the people to eat and celebrate Gray Fox's dedication. Raven submitted to his Elder and walked away and began ranting about what he seen on this baby. The demons began poking at him and scorning him for his mess up.

This made him so made that he screamed at them to leave him alone for now. They left but said they would be back because he was their slave to do their bidding as they want. As Morning Dove took her son back to the hut, and the celebration kept going for over 2 hours. As evening came to an end, Spotted Wolf made his way back to his hut to find his wife and son soundly asleep. He put more wood on the fire making sure it was warm enough for them. He laid down beside Morning Dove and so gently kissed her on the cheek. He told her that he loved her and was so proud of her and their son at the ceremony today. She rolled over and put her hand on his face and told him that he was going to make a great father to their son and raise him to be a great warrior like him.

They both gently kissed their son goodnight and the baby so softly whimpered like a puppy. They both grinned and fell asleep from another day of being proud parents. At Raven's hut he was walking back and forth trying to figure this strange thing that happened to him when blowing the smoke upon the baby. He had never had this happen before and he was going to find out why and how to overcome it with his spells.

As he finally laid down for the night, he just knew that vision he had many moons ago was real and that surely the spirits would not lead him wrong. He began to chant to himself so that his nerves would settle down and get some much-needed sleep. Unaware that the four demons were standing by him, and planning what the next step was to get Raven to do their bidding. Yet they were very nervous about the heavenly angel that was assigned to the baby. They had never seen this angel in the area before and wondered about the divine purpose he had here.

Chapter 4

The Storm Approaching

It was in the spring of 1782 in the Chota village was like any other day when a French fur trader named Francois came to the camp to talk to Spotted Wolf and his leaders. Spotted Wolf knew him very well and had been friends since their youth and always treated him like a blood brother.

As the man got closer, Spotted Wolf noticed from a distance that he did not have his pack horses as usual with plenty of white man goods. The brave escorted the French man to their Chief Elders hut. They both greeted each other with a hug and Francois told Spotted Wolf that he needed to get all his leaders together for a meeting about something very important to their tribe.

So, all the leaders came and sat down in Spotted Wolf's lodge and welcomed his old friend. They passed the peace pipe around and got comfortable and was ready to hear what the white fur trader had to say. The man pauses for a moment and looked towards the ceiling of the hut and asked if he could speak honestly with them. Spotted Wolf told him that he should always feel led to tell the truth. For they had known each other too long by now to do otherwise. François took the pipe one more time and took a puff and blew out the smoke very slowly.

Then Francois started telling them that he had to come to the Cherokee nation and the need to share something bad that was coming. Then he started to tell them that there is a vast number of white men coming across the big pond and making many new villages and spreading all over the native's land. And now they are expanding towards the west and taking more land from the Indians who were living there by birthright.

He paused for a minute and told them that King George II of the great country called the United Kingdom of Britain. Has now plans to try uniting certain tribes to fight against the new Pilgrims that have been here in this country a little over a hundred years. Spotted Wolf stopped him for a minute and asked why does this concern the Cherokee nation? He told the man that the Cherokee nation has been approached by the Red Coats to help them to fight the new settlers. Plus, they can keep their land by joining with King George II for helping to fight the new settlers. But they have chosen to reject King George II offer. Why couldn't they both live on this land? The land is massive and there is enough room for the Indians and the white man.

The man stood upright and told Spotted Wolf this was nothing but a lie from King George II. The white man and his religion wanted this entire land for themselves because they believed this was their New Promised Land and their true followers. The fur trader told them that the white man only wants to take this land from the all Indians and make them extinct because they were savages and heathens. The whole room of leaders started to protest in what they just heard this man saying.

Spotted Wolf raised his hands in motions and the room grew quite to hear their Chief Elder speak with wisdom. François then stood and said that he had found out the plan to get rid of all the Indians. Not only in war but spread a deadly disease that will wipe all the

Indians out. Spotted Wolf asked the man what kind of disease is this? The man said that he has been in this country for 50 years and knows how the Indians are and how healthy they are. He folded his arms and said that this disease is a killer among white man and that they have brought it across the big pond, and they plan to spread it among the Indians.

Spotted Wolf looked at the ground for a while and with a sad look on his face; he asked how they were going to do this? The man told them more than likely they will put this disease on blankets or clothing when they are handed out to the tribes. Or they will send in traders who have this disease and the Indians can catch it by contact with their skin. Then Francois with stern look in face told the leaders not to let any white man in their camp at all or accept any blankets or clothing from them.

Spotted Wolf ask how can they catch this disease by those who are infected by skin contact? The trader told him that it was the persons bodily fluids like spit or sores that carries the disease. Then François told him that the all camps needs to be on watch for any white man or his tangible goods. Then with a grim look on his face, he told him that disease is so deadly it can kill hundreds of people in a very short time. Then Spotted Wolf asked how can they know if a person has this disease? He told them that they can have skin blisters on their bodies. The trader then hung his head and with tears told him that already there has been an entire village of Native Indians that have been completely wiped out.

Spotted Wolf then grabbed his friend and told him thank you so much for bringing this devastating news to his camp. He told him that he will make sure that his whole camp will be warned about this and be careful of running into other Indians and the white men. Francois hug him back and told him that he must go and warn the others camps of Cherokee of this deadly disease. They both said their farewells and Spotted Wolf knew that this might be the last time he will see his old friend again.

All the leaders then began to talk among themselves and knew that from now on, they must not allow any white man into their camp. Then Raven spoke out with an angry voice and said that now you can see the proof that this is the reason why the white man cannot be trusted in anything they say or do. Therefore, we must wipe them out and send them back to their own country across the big pond. Some of the leaders cried out in a war cry and was ready to take vengeance against the white man.

Spotted Wolf told them to settle down because the truth is that there are way too many white men to fight against. One of the leaders spoke up and said that there were a little over 10, 000 Cherokees. Along with the Chickasaw, Choctaws, Creek and Seminoles. With all these tribes, they had over 25,000 people.

Spotted Wolf once again told them to settle down and that they must be prepare for this dark storm that is coming their way. They all agreed, yet some of them were thinking to themselves that they must go now and wipe out the white man and then there would be no deadly disease. They all left Spotted Wolf's hut and went back to their own huts carrying a heavy heart of what they just heard in the meeting. Morning Dove came from her sister-in-law's hut and had a big smile on her face as she approached her husband.

She seen the grim look on his face and asked him what was wrong? He gave her a fake smile and asked her what she was so happy about? Morning Dove began to tell him that his baby brother was expecting his first child and would be born close to summer. He told her that was great news and that he is so happy for them. Then she stopped him in his tracks and asked what was really going on with the meeting?

He asked her to sit down with their young child and began to tell her what the bad news was all about. She sat there for a minute and was so amazed that this is from the vision she had before their child was born. She started to cry, and Spotted Wolf tried to comfort her in her sorrow. After a moment she gathered herself and began to tell him what had happened to her before a year before she got pregnant with their son.

An angel had showed her a vision of the valley of dead Indians and her having a son. All this was going to take place after he was born. He just sat back against the wall and was shocked to hear what had happened to her. He then asked her why she didn't share this with him?

She told him that she was sorry and that she was not sure how to handle the vision that was given to her. Spotted Wolf grabbed her hand and told her that he understands how she feels and that he has known for a long time that her special connection to the Great Creator was a heritage passed down through her mother and many generations before.

He then told her that he longs too for his nation to come back into the old ways of their ancestors in the land far away. And that too many tribes have their lost their true heritage for too many years. But for now, they had to deal with this deadly disease that will come to kill way too many Indians. Morning Dove spoke up and said that the angel told her that their family would be safe because their son had a great mission to reach their people and the other four tribes in the region.

As they continued to talk about the coming danger, Gabriel suddenly stands at the entrance to their hut. Spotted Wolf was startled at first and then realized that this was a holy messenger from their Great Creator. He bowed to the angel and Gabriel told him to stand up because he was not worthy of his praise.

As he stood up with Morning Dove, Gabriel once again gave the message that their family would be safe during this great ordeal. But that sadly too many of their brethren would lose their lives because of this disease that the white man is bringing. Yet also many white men and their families would also lose their lives to this disease.

Then Gabriel looked over at the 1.5 year old baby boy and told his parents that heaven would protect this child from this disease and the evil spirits that would do him great harm and try to kill him if possible. Then he told Spotted Wolf that he needs to be careful of Raven because he's the very one that wants to kill their son. Both Spotted Wolf and Morning Dove just looked at each other with disbelief in what Gabriel had just said about Raven! They commented that this could not be true at all. Gabriel looked right into their eyes and said he was not capable of lying.

Gabriel then told them that for the next six months it will be hard for the Cherokee nation and the other 4 nations as well. Just believe what your Great Creator has told you and that He will keep His promises to you and your son.

Then he hugs them and said farewell and that the other angel named Michael will protect their son and them during this horrible event. And just like he came, he went the same way. They both hugged each other and felt comforted in what the Holy Angel had just told them.

They both agreed that they would not let Raven know what he is up too. With his evil plans was for their son. It was time to go to bed with their son and get a good night sleep. They kissed each other and their son and drew the furs over them, it was going be a cold night for them. It had been about 6 months since they received the word from Gabriel about the deadly disease. Now the word was getting around that the white men were building settlements about 30 miles from the Cherokee camp. Every once and awhile they would see trappers and they did not come close to their camps. Spotted Wolf had heard that many of his fellow natives were being affected by the white men disease. This made him very worried and yet he trusted what Gabriel had promised them. Spotted Wolf had sent out some of his scouts to watch their borders and report back to him when the white man was getting too close.

Little did he know that some of his fellow Cherokees had gone beyond their borders and came in contact with the white man. He had heard that they wanted to trade their furs for the white man's goods like blankets, pans and certain accessories.

Of course, this made him very upset but how would he know which ones did this. Then the day came when he got word that in the main village where the Head Elder lived. That many Indians became very sick and that many died from an unknown disease. The Holy man started to proclaim that this was the punishment of the Great Spirit because they somehow broke their traditions and laws.

In the next few weeks, Spotted Wolf began to hear more reports of his brothers were dying and many of them were killing themselves because their skin became deformed. It was not until this disease became like a wild fire spreading all over the Tennessee Valley. On a certain day Morning Dove went out to her usual prayer place along with 2 personal guards to protect her from any harm to her and her four-year-old son. Gray Fox was walking by her and he was excited to go with his mom to her prayer place. He kept chattering and chattering about the barren trees and bushes because of being the winter time. Today was not too cold and Morning Dove needed to go to her prayer place. For it had been awhile since she had come to her holy place. As they continued down the pathway with the two warriors not too far behind them. Suddenly a rabbit ran across their path and Gray Fox began to follow it. She grabbed his hands quickly and told him to stop chasing the rabbit.

Finally, they came to a little clearing in the woods and the little hut was still there. She sighed with a relief that no animals had destroyed it. Morning Dove told the two guards to stand just in the tree line and she would come out when she was done. As she and her son got inside the little hut, she built a small fire to keep them warm. The 2 guards watched the smoke begin to rise above the hut while they made their own campfire.

As Morning Dove stoked the fire and told Gray Fox not sit too close to the fire. He asked his mom why are we here? Then he mention that he is hungry and kept rambling on like a four year old.

She handed him a buffalo jerky and told him to eat it and be quiet cause mommy needed to pray to her Creator. Of course, he began to ask who this Creator was and when would he show up in the hut. Morning Dove just laughed at him and told him that he is the Great Spirit that all Indians pray too. That he is everywhere and in all the creation on earth.

He started to ask something else when she gave him the look that he knew he better be quiet right now. So, he began to chew the jerky and said he was thirsty. She grabbed her water bag and handed it to him. Now she then put her finger on her lips and said be quiet now!

About 30 minutes into her prayer she notices that her precious son was fast asleep holding the piece of jerky in his hands. As she began to start praying with her heavenly language, all of a sudden, a bright light showed up in the hut. At first, she was startled but realized what was getting ready to happen. Gabriel appeared before her in a sitting position in front of her. He greeted her with peace and that he had some things to talk to her about. She told him that her vision and warning had come to pass and that there was much death among the Cherokees and other tribes. He just bowed his head and sighed for a moment and told her that the Heavens was quite aware of what was happening to the Natives.

She began to cry softly and ask why did this have to happen to her people? Gabriel reminded her that this was the plot of the evil one and along with many white men to get rid of the natives. They wanted their lands and they did not care how they did it. He told her that there will be wars between them and other tribes that have sold their souls to the white man and his religion of peace. She stopped him and said that in no way is this peace when man tries to kill his fellow man for land and greed!

She said that she knew that one must defend their lives from any one that would try to kill them. But to do it in such an evil way is not the way of the Great Creator. Gabriel agree with her that this is true, but the heart of man is wicked, and they have left the ways of the Creator who made them. Then Gabriel told her that when her son reaches the age of 18. He will become a mighty warrior and become the best archer and skilled hunter among the Cherokees. Then when he enters into his prayer hut to get his own vision. There is where he will encounter the Great Sprit and even his son. To learn his divine calling for his own people and those who will listen to him.

Then he grabbed Morning Dove's hand and told her that she needed to start training him in the ways of the Great Creator and prepare him for when he is 14 years old.

She promised him as long as she was alive that she will teach the true ways of the Great Creator. About that time Gray Wolf began to wake up and Gabriel disappeared from her sight. Of course, he resumes eating his jerky and wanting something to drink as usual. She just laughs and said that it was time go back home and there were chores to be done before night fall.

He started raising his hands and gave out the best war cry he could. She laughed again and told him to get up because they are going home. As she came out of her prayer hut, she notices that 2 Indians were leaning up against a tree sleeping. Gray Fox began to howl like a wolf and startled them. Morning Dove had a good laugh and asked why they fell asleep on the job? They both told her that they were sorry and that somehow, they got really sleepy. She told them it was okay but not to let it happen again. She then winks and promised them that she would not tell her husband about what they did. They both thanked her and promised it would never happen again.

They began to walk back to the camp and Gray Fox was trying to catch a rabbit a little too far from his mom. One of the guards ran after him and picked him up while he was screaming mommy! As they kept walking back to the camp, Morning Dove still had wondered if old Scar Face would show up like in the vision she had before Gray Fox was born. As they arrived in the camp, she was quite relieved that she had not encountered the old bear.

Spotted Wolf greeted her at the entrance of their hut with a kiss and asked if everything went okay during her prayer time? She just kissed him back and said it went well and that Gray Fox was really acting like a four-year-old. They got settled for the night and wondered what tomorrow would bring in their life.

For this year had been devastating to the Cherokee Nations and other tribes from the small pox outbreak. As Spotted Wolf gave his wife and son a kiss; he promised her that the Cherokees would arise again from these ashes and would be great again. She grabbed his hand and told him that she knew the promises of the Great Creator would be with them and in the years to come.

They both turned over and went to sleep not knowing that Raven was pacing back and forth in his hut chanting his spells upon Gray Fox. The four demons that were assigned to him kept putting their crooked fingers into his soul and causing him to go into his trance.

Raven just had to get the very wisdom from the great warriors of the past to get Gray Fox to become their savior from the white men. No matter what it took, he was going to succeed in his mission. But for the next few years he had plenty of time to try and figure out his evil plan to make Gray Fox the mighty warrior that would kill and drive out the white man off their land. And if this did not work for him. Then he had no choice but to kill Gray Fox's dream and end his life for good.

Yet he pondered what do with this evil spirit that was protecting Gray Fox. Once again, he fell into his trance hoping to get his guidance on this mission of making Gray Fox the mighty warrior for his people. The four demons were dancing around Raven's body chanting their curses at him, knowing that Raven's soul and spirit belonged to them. They were the puppet masters of this man who was greatly deceived by these spirits.

Finally, he quit shaking and got on his knees and sat before the fire. Then one of the demons appeared in front of him dressed like a holy man from the past. He began to tell Raven to keep on chanting his spells on Gray Fox. Yet the time will come that he will send Raven a young holy man to help him on this mission.

Then the demon pointed his fingers at Raven's face and told him not to fail him. Gray Fox must be stopped from his holy mission of reaching his fellow Indians with the message of righteousness. Raven began to ask the demon a question when suddenly his body was thrown down face first. The demon screamed aloud and vanished out of sight.

Raven's entire body went limp and soon he fell asleep from the ordeal with the demon. The four demons were charged with excitement knowing that their mission was on the right path.

Chapter 5

Scar-Face

It had been over 14 years since the deadly plague of small pox had done great damage to the natives of this new promised land. It seemed more than ever that the number of the white man grew beyond the imagination of the natives. All they knew was this enemy was growing stronger every day and that their sacred land was falling into the hands of men that did not have respect or understanding how holy this land was.

It was at this time that Gray Fox began his training with other young men his age for their manhood as mighty warriors for the Cherokee Nation. This was every young warrior's dream to be finally recognized as warriors for this great nation. Gray Fox was so ready to start his training and was wanting to show his father how much he had learned from him. Every afternoon all the young warriors would gather outside the camp to shoot their bow and arrows and making a precise hit on the target.

They even had the luxury of having the white man long stick (rifle) to make them a better warrior against the white man.

Gray Fox and his cousin Running Bear were always in competition with each other since they learned to walk. Even though Gray Fox was 1.5 years older then Running Bear, he always was the faster one of the two.

Sometimes their competitive spirits caused them to get into a lot of fights; yet they acted like brothers and always made up. Both became very accurate with their bow and arrows. But unlike Gray Fox's father, they had a new weapon to train with and they wanted to become just as accurate as their bows. The Indians call this weapon; Long Stick (musket rifle) in which the white man had brought over from the great pond in the mid 1600's.

This weapon was more powerful than their bows because it could hit a target at 100 yards with a lot of practice. So, when they went hunting for game, they soon learned that they had a great advantage over the animals as far as distance goes. Gray Fox loved how the long stick felt in his hands and that he wanted to become the best in his tribe.

The young warriors began to learn how to hunt with them and with their bows and arrows. Each warrior already been taught by their fathers at an early age. By the time the training was finished, Gray Fox became one of the best in the whole camp. Now the first part of their training for manhood as a warrior was completed. It was time to go into their second part of training in which was the spiritual part that was needed to become a great warrior. This was the time where each young warrior would go off into the woods and build their own sweat hut and get their holy vision of their destiny as a warrior for the Cherokee nation. There was no set time for them, and they were not allowed to come back until they received their vision from the spirits of past warriors.

As Gray Fox prepared to make his journey the next two mornings, he was called by his mother to come and go with her to her prayer hut. At first, he told her that he did not want to go but wanted to go with Running Bear. She just gave him that look that only a mother can give to her children. Of course, he knew then he better go with her to her place of prayer. As usual they had two guards follow them to the place where it seemed that The Kingdom of Heaven came down to meet with mortal man.

As they got closer to the hut, the two guards went to their normal resting place. Morning Dove and the young warrior went inside the hut to have their time of prayer. Gray Fox kept thinking that he would rather be with Running Bear and enjoy his company before they made his spiritual journey,

He kept scratching at the ground with a stick while his mother began to talk to him. She then suddenly grabbed the stick from him and told him that she was serious and wanted to share something with him before he left on his spiritual journey. He apologized to his mother and told her that she has his full attention on this important matter.

She began to remind him all the things she had shared with him over the last 14 years. Morning Dove told him that he was coming of age to really understand the truth about the Great Creator and His son **Y**o-**H**e-Wa**H**-Si (Jesus). That he had a divine purpose on this earth to the Cherokee Nation and the other four tribes. She explained to him that she will not be around forever and that the Spirit of the Great Creator would lead and guide him through his life.

Gray Fox told his mother that he understood her and yet he wanted to become a great warrior and to help drive out the white man from their land. She gently grabbed his hands and told him that the white men have come and will never leave this land of theirs. Then Gray Fox said that it would be a great honor as a warrior to die for this cause.

She then told him to stop it and that she was promised by an angel of his birth when she was barren. That he would become a prophet unto his people and that it is settled. Gray Fox then asked her what is a angel and where do they live. She then proceeded to him that an angel was a holy messenger from the Great Creator of the heavenly spirit realm.

That spirit realm was where the Kingdom of the Great Creator and His son; **Y**o-**H**e-**W**a**H**-si (Jesus) lived to rule over the earth. It was His son that died for mankind so that man could be in the right relationship with the Great Creator. Gray Fox then asked her what this angel looked like and was he an Indian like him? She laughed for a bit and told him that the Holy Angels were not mortal man, and they could take on the appearance of a man of any race. They were very tall and yet they can appear the size of a normal man. Gray Fox then asked her if this angel was like a shape-shiftier among the Indians? Morning Dove told him in no way were they like the certain warriors who worship certain creatures. And taking on their spirit and having the ability to change into that animal form.

She told him that this was an evil practice that the Indians were taught by their ancestors many moons ago. Their purpose was to terrorize their enemy's and even kill them if necessary. Then they would turn back into their human form. She then told him that this practice took a heavy toll upon that person's human body. Because the Great Creator did not create man for this evil practice.

She told him that there was an evil force upon this earth to cause man to turn from their Creator and to worship spirits that roam this great land. Gray Fox told her that he was beginning to understand what his mother was telling him about the Great Creator and His Holy messenger. He could tell that she was so serious in what she was saying. Her eyes told him everything and he could see that she was telling him the truth. He knew that his mother would never lie to him. He once again apologized to his mom and that he would honor her wish and promised that his heart would be open to her dreams for him and his life. Suddenly they heard a scream of someone shouting and the sound of a bear. Morning Dove knew in her spirit heart then that her vision she had at the birth of Gray Fox was coming to pass after all these years.

They both got out of the hut to see one of the guards running toward where the scream was coming from. They both heard the loud roar coming from the north of their position. Then heard the scream of death and then a great roar from a bear. Morning Dove knew then that one of the guards had been killed by Scar Face. She watch as the other guard came running to her and telling her that they needed to go back to the camp as fast as possible. As Morning Dove began to turn and run, Gray Fox told her that he would protect her no matter what. Then another scream broke out about 30 yards from them in the woods. She knew then that Scar-face had killed the other guard. Gray Fox had forgotten his long stick, so he took up his bow and arrow and was ready to face the black bear. His mom told him that the bow and arrow would not kill the bear and to start running back to the camp. She knew they had a head start on the bear being about 30 yards from him. As they began run, Gray Fox kept his weapon ready to use and began to run after his mom. As they began to come to the turn in the path to the camp suddenly out of nowhere Scar-face was standing on his legs making his vicious war sound.

Morning Dove was startled to see him in front of her. She knew in her spirit that the evil spirits that possessed the bear had him supernaturally place him in their path. Gray Fox could not believe how fast the bear ran and that somehow, he had outrun them to this place. He was amazed how big the black bear was. He was taller than any bear he had ever seen in his life. The bear was at least 6ft tall and his black fur smelled like something he had never ever smelled before. He then noticed the big scar that was under his right eye and even other scar that covered his body. Then Scarface shook his head back and forth as if he is warning them of his attack. Gray Fox then decided that because the bear was so huge and very fat he knew in his heart that his arrows would not stop him. Then he decided he would run around the bear in circles so that his mom could escape from the bear. Gray Fox let out a war cry and began to run around the bear as fast as he could. His mom wanted him to stop except she remembered the vision that she had many moons ago. The bear became so mad that Gray Fox was running in circles around him. As Gray Fox began to go around one more time, the bear decided to go towards Morning Dove. As the bear stood up again, he made his way towards Morning Dove.

Gray Fox then ran and got in front of his mom and drew his bow and arrow. The bear was only 15 yards from his next victim. Gray Fox drew back his arrow as much as he could and took aim at the bear. Morning Dove began to pray in her prayer language when suddenly Michael the warring angel was standing behind Gray Fox.

She knew that her son was really scared and that he wanted to show his mom that he had great courage as a young warrior. She then watches the bear standing tall on his hind feet coming to make his kill. As Gray Fox drew back harder the arrow, he could feel someone's hand on his and helping to point the arrow in the right direction of the bear. Then he held his breath and let go of the arrow to reach its target and hoping it makes it mark on the bear. He closed his eyes for a second and watched the arrow makes its way towards the black bear. Suddenly it hit the bear and he screamed out loudly as the arrow pierced his heart. He screams one more time and fell to the ground just in front of his mother.

Gray Fox screamed out with a loud war cry because he just brought down the famous black bear known in the region. His mom also made a loud war cry and began to raise her hands towards the heavens. She was giving praise to her Great Creator for this victory.

As she brought her hands down, she could see Michael standing over Scarface. She then stretches out her hands over the bear and rebuked the evil spirits in the name of **Yo-He-WaH**-si (Jesus) Then it was like her eyes were opened to the spirit realm and untold number of demons was leaving the old bear's body. They were screaming as if they were in terror of someone. Suddenly the bears fur and appearance began to change truly as an old natural bear that he was created as. The old bear took his last breath and with that he closed his eyes for good. Gray Fox and his mom picked up their knives and began to skin the hide of his grand trophy. He couldn't wait to show his father what he did to protect his mom from the great Scarface. They began to walk back to camp and was greeted by his father and what seemed to be the whole camp. The great news of Gray Fox killing Scarface had traveled to other clans of the Cherokee Nation.

For this was a time of great celebration among the Cherokee nation. For too many years Scarface had become a great nuisance to the Cherokee and other tribes. Then you could see all the young and old warriors standing around Gray Fox as he was telling his story how he ran around the bear so fast so that he could protect his mom from the vicious bear.

All the warriors were standing by him were celebrating and shouting with great joy and yelling out their war cry. As they were all yelling; Gray Fox kept thinking to himself how he felt the presence of someone's hands touching his as he shot the arrow with his eyes closed.

The celebration continued into the night until they became tired from eating, drinking and telling his story. Then they all began heading back to their own lodges. As Gray Fox came to his family hut, his father told him that he was very proud of him of protecting his mother. Gray Fox told him it was nothing and then his father put his hands on his shoulder and the young warrior began to tell his dad that he was very scared when all this happened!

Spotted Wolf explained to him that it was good to be afraid of your enemy but learn to overcome that fear. Then Gray Fox proceeded to tell him that he had felt a hand on his as he shot the arrow and that his eyes were closed. Spotted Wolf laughed for a moment and said that it sounds like he had divine intervention. Of course, this made Gray Fox think of what his mom had told him about the Great Creator and His son and the angels.

He then stepped outside and turned to look into the starry night and began to thank The Great Creator for helping him to kill the old bear. As Gray Fox re-entered their lodge, Morning Dove came up to him and hugged him as tight as she could. Thanking him for being a brave warrior and what had happened today that was foretold by an angel before he was born. After she told him everything, she got ready to lay down for the night. She gave him a kiss that only mothers knows how to do. Gray Fox parents went to bed while he laid there thinking about what his mom had shared with him.

For the first time in his entire life of what his mom had been teaching and sharing with him about the ways of their ancestors and the Great Creator and **YoHeWaH**-si (Jesus) started to make sense to him. He quietly got up and went outside their lodge and looked into the sky and seen the stars a different way than before.

In a couple of days was when he would venture out to find his own prayer hut. In order to find his own divine destiny as a warrior of the Cherokee nation.

Chapter 6

The Prayer Chamber

That day finally came since Gray Fox
had killed Scarface the legendary black
bear. As the sun began to peek over the
ridges, the fresh snow was the sign that
winter was coming upon this region of
Appalachia Mt. The camp was alive as all
the young warriors were telling their
families goodbye for this holy adventure of
their young lives.

Gray Fox hugged his father and told him
that he would make him proud as his son
and to the family lineage of great Chiefs
and Warriors. Spotted Wolf looked into his
sons' eyes and told him that he had
always been proud of him since the day he
was born. And he too would pray for him
in this great journey of life that he is
embarking on as a young warrior.

Then it was Morning Dove's turn to say
goodbye to her son. She began to ask him
if he had everything he needed for the trip
and that if wanted to; he could use her
prayer hut. Then she started to cry for
him, and he quickly told her that he was
not a little boy anymore. She then told
him that he will always be her little boy.

He told her to quit her crying and that he is becoming a man after this prayer ritual is over. He smiled at her and appreciated her offer, yet he had to find his own special prayer place for his life as a mighty warrior. Morning Dove told him that she understood him and that she would be praying that he would have the encounters with the Holy Angels as she did as a young girl and a woman. He gave them both a hug one more time and started to head east of where his mom's prayer hut was.

As he started, he saw Running Bear running up to him to say goodbye. They both hugged and Gray Fox told him to look out for his mom. Running Bear beat his chest and proclaimed it would be a great honor to watch over his parents.

Gray Fox turned to see his mom crying and yelled back at her that he was a man now and that he would come back as a mighty warrior. Morning Dove told him that she loved him and under her breath, she asks the Great Creator to keep his promise to her. Then she heard this small voice telling her that he will be okay and that he will come back a changed young man.

Gray Fox was excited but also real nervous of this most important trip of his young life. He remembers hearing his father's story when he went to his prayer lodge and the vision that he was given to him by a great warrior spirit. He followed the same path that went to his mother's prayer lodge that passed the spot where he killed Scarface the great black bear. He still could not believe that one arrow killed the old bear yet knowing that he had divine help from above.

He just stood there and stared at that famous spot for a minute and knew it was time to find his own prayer hut. He had gone about 5 miles beyond his mother's prayer hut and saw a small cave opening on a hill that had a lot of trees and brush surrounding it. He felt that he had an over look of the area to see if any dangerous animals or humans were approaching him. So, he checks the small cave out and was surprised how big it was inside. He could see that some animal had made its home there, but it's been awhile since they were there. So, he figured he was safe for now and it was time to gather sticks to make the fire for this most holy ceremony of any young warrior's life.

He decided to cut down more branches to help hide the cave opening. After he had gathered everything, he needed for his fire it was time to start it and get settled for the night. He was so anxious and yet nervous to get started to receive his divine vision from the great spirit warriors of his ancestors. He grabbed some deer jerky and was chewing on it when he noticed that it seemed like he was sitting on some kind of a mound.

So, he decided to make the fire brighter to see what the mound was. He saw that the length of it must have been at least 10ft and the width about the size of three men. His curiosity really got aroused that this mound was not normal and could not have been a burial of a person. For he knew that in his native culture, they always buried a love one on top of a wooden type of scaffolding and raised it in the air about 6 feet.

So that ruled out it was an Indian grave and he wondered if there were any other mounds like this in the cave. Yet he knew if this is a burial site of a man that it was wrong to disturb the spirit of a dead man. So, he quickly got off the mound and stood up to see if there were any other mounds in this small cave. As he took a torch to look around, he was astonished how big the cave was. It had to go back at least another 50 yards. He then saw some writings on the walls of the cave. He could tell that these were very old drawings of Indians way before the time that he was aware of. As he looked closer, he could see what seemed to be a group of Indians with spears looking towards an object in front of them.

Then too his great surprise, he notices a drawing of seem to be a large man that was way taller than the Indians. As he looked closer at the drawing of what seemed to be a giant man, he could not believe his eyes. For the drawing of this giant man showed that he had reddish hair and was carrying a large spear himself.

He rubbed his eyes and held the torch closer to the drawing of the giant man with reddish hair. Then suddenly he remembered the stories his mom had told him in early childhood about the giants that roamed this area and they were called "Cloud-Eaters." For there were great wars that took place between the Indians and the Cloud-Eaters.

Surely, he thought this was nothing but an old legend that has been passed around for hundreds of years. Besides anybody could have drawn these drawings of the giants and was playing a joke on who ever found it. So, he decided to go back to the mound and was thinking that his mom would not have lied about this legend!

Then he looked at the mound and decided to dig and see what lay below this huge mound. So, he started to dig and had not dug very deep when he noticed a bone of a hand. As he dug a little more, he notices that this bone of a hand was not the normal size of a man. He could not believe this eyes that he was holding a human hand that was four times bigger than his.

His curiosity got to him so bad that he started to dig faster and began uncovering what seemed to be the bones of a Cloud-Eater. He was startled to see that this giant man had six toes and six fingers. He kept telling himself this was a dream and that he needed to wake up from this horrible dream! Finally, he was done digging and there lay before him the bones of at least a 9ft person.

This was too much for him and he hurried out of the cave. His body was shaking with unbelief, but the true reality was the stories his mom had told was really true and that her faith in the Great Creator was real. Then he just looked up into the darkness of night and saw the stars shinning like never before to him. He lifted his hands towards heaven and cried out to the Great **YeHehaWaH**eha (He who Creates) that if He was truly real to his mom; then he must know him as she did.

He just gazed at the bright stars when suddenly he felt a warm breeze blow into his face. Then out of nowhere, this light began to shine from a distance from him. Yet this light was moving towards him very fast and he began to fear that a bad spirit was coming to harm him. He closed his eyes for a second and then the whole area he was standing in was engulfed with this bright light.

He fell to the ground and cried out so that the evil spirit would not harm him. He heard a voice calling him by his name and saying Be Not Afraid; for I am the Holy Messenger (Angel) from the Great Creator to bring to you His Holy message. Gray Fox opened his eyes to see a man shinning like the morning sun. So, he covered his eyes and then the bright light disappeared like it came. Gray Fox noticed that the man was dressed in a peculiar outfit that he had never seen before. Then the man spoke to him and told Gray Fox that his name was Gabriel. Then the Angel began to tell Gray Fox that he was the same angel that was sent to his mom to let her know that she would conceive and bring forth a son to her and his father. For it was time to let him know what his divine destiny was and purpose in life.

Then Gray Fox just stood there for a moment and could not believe what he was seeing standing before him this night. Then Gabriel told him to touch him and to see that he was not an evil spirit but that he just as real as him. Gray Fox grabbed his hands and felt such a great peace that he had never known before in his life. He then knew that this was not a bad dream but felt such a great honor to have this holy messenger come to him.

Gabriel then told Gray Fox to sit down and that there was much to share with him this night. Gray Fox could not believe how quiet it was in the woods at this time.

There were not any sounds coming from the usual night animals. It was like all creations were silent to hear the holy messenger bring forth holy words from the Great Creator. As Gray Fox got situated to hear from Gabriel, he noticed that the angel pointed his finger towards the ground in front of him and suddenly a warm fire was blazing.

Once again Gray Fox could not believe what he just saw, but this had to be an angel from Heaven. He even thought about Raven who did not have this kind of demonstration of power. As they both sat there, Gabriel began to tell him the story how the Great Creator had sent his only Son to die for mankind sins so that they could have the proper relationship with Him. When he had finished the story, he told Gabriel that this was the same story his mom had taught him at an early age of his childhood.

Then Gray Fox told him that their holy medicine man Raven has told everybody in their camp that he was born to become the greatest warrior for the Cherokee nation. That his purpose was to drive out and kill the white man and send them back across the big pond where they came from. Gabriel then told Gray Fox that this was not the purpose for him to be born and that Raven was being driven by wicked evil spirits and have convinced him that you must die. Gray Fox sat bewildered about that because he thought that Raven loved him as Spotted Wolf's son.

Gabriel put his hand on Gray Fox's shoulder and told him that there would be many over his life time that wanted him to be killed. All because he was challenging their holy traditions of the spirits they worship. Gray Fox looked at him and said that they must know the real truth of their Creator.

Then Gray Fox looked back at the cave and began to ask Gabriel about the giant bones he had found and the drawing on the walls. Gabriel paused for a minute with a smile on his face and began to tell him the story about the giants (Cloud-Eaters) and how they came on this earth and mated with the woman and produced the giants who lived on the Earth for 500 years. He told Gray Fox at first the giants lived in peace among mankind for a period of time.

Then the giants began to eat man's food source and causing a famine among mankind. He then told him that the time came because of the great famine that the giants began to eat the flesh of humans. Gray Fox could not believe what he was hearing. Gabriel told him that man had some success of killing the giants when they banned together as one body.

But yet the giants were too much for them and that The Great Creator commanded the Watchers (fallen angels) to kill their own off-springs and not to let one survive. He said this is the reason why The Creator caused the great flood for the wickedness of men whose hearts turned against Him. Plus, the animal's bloodline had been corrupted by the Watchers and thus causing very strange breed of animals to be on this earth.

Gabriel told Gray Fox that the Great Creator had one family who had not turned their backs on Him through this whole ordeal. That they built a great boat that carried animals that were not corrupted and the eight people who would start a new world for mankind. Gabriel then told him that before the great flood took place, that all the known land was one great land before the floods separated them. This is how the giants had come to this land and that hundreds of them had lived and were killed and buried in this land. Gabriel then asked Gray Fox to follow him into the cave and to show him something. As soon as they entered the cave, the whole place lit up from the presence of Gabriel. Gray Fox was still in awe about this angel and the power he possesses.

They walked to the wall to look at the painting and then Gabriel explained to him that his ancestors tried their best to get rid of the giants. He said that they had killed some, but it took the Watchers to kill all of them. Gabriel then told him that these bones of a giant was one that Gray Fox forefathers had killed and buried the bones that lay here. So Gray Fox looked closer at the painting and seen an Indian with others killing the giant. He said that this must be my forefather. Gabriel said yes and said that they had a great celebration that day when they killed this particular giant.

Gray Fox then realized for the first time in his young life that his moms stories were true and that there is a Creator and his angels that are watching over him and his family. He just stood there for a moment and then got on his hands and knees and cried. While he was crying, he asked the angels what he must do to live and walk in the ways of his Creator? Then Gabriel told him again about the Creator Son coming to earth to die for the human race and was raised from the dead so that the humans can have a personal relationship with Him.

Gray Fox started to feel a great conviction in his soul that he must accept this message and receive the very love of the son of the Creator. Then Gray Fox asked Gabriel what was the Creator Son's name? Gabriel told him that his mom knows his name very well and that his name is; **YoHeWaH**-si (Jesus) Gray Fox then got on his knees and raised his hands high into the air and called out to **YoHeWaH**-si to save him! Just as his words were finished, he felt this unusual feeling of what seemed to be an oil dripping down onto his head.

It felt so peaceful to him and a joy that he had never known before. He just couldn't get over the peace that he felt, and he knew that this is how his mom feels knowing the great Creator. He knew then that this was what he needed in his life and that now he has a purpose in life. Gray Fox just wanted to make his parents proud as a warrior and now a true believer of the Great Creator. Yet he couldn't get over the love that engulfed his whole soul and being. He then turns to Gabriel and hugged him and told him how grateful he was to come and show him the true way of knowing **YoHeWaH**-si (Jesus) and the Great Creator.

Gabriel told him that now he must spend time in his prayer chamber and get ready to receive power from on high to help him to live a righteous life before his Creator. Plus, that Great Spirit will show him the great path that he must take this day forward and for the rest of his life. Even this great mission that he will take will be challenging and even dangerous in this calling. Gray Fox wanted to ask him what his calling was, but Gabriel told him that he must spend time in his prayer chamber to get the answer he needed.

Gray Fox turned around for a second and was getting ready to ask the angel another question when he noticed that Gabriel was gone.

Then his eyes once again turned to look at the paintings on the walls of the cave. He thought to himself that it must have been exciting to live in those days and see the Cloud-Eaters roaming this land. Yet Gray Fox knew it was time to get settled down and start his ceremony for his manhood and to become a mighty warrior for his people and now for his Savior and Messiah. He had so many questions about his Messiah and was eager to learn more about Him. All this excitement got to him and it was getting late and soon he fell asleep.

Little did he know that he was about to have a Holy encounter with his new-found Messiah. About three hours into his sleep, he thought he heard a man calling his name a distance away and then turned over on his side. Once again, he heard his name called and woke up with his knife in his hand. He then looked around and did not see no one in the cave with him.

He then grabbed his blanket and pulled it over his head. Once again, he heard his name called and decided that someone had to be in the cave with him. He cried out asking who was there? But yet no response except some bats making their way out of the cave. Gray Fox just knew he was hearing things and decided to move closer to the walls of the cave. Just as he closed his eyes, he heard his name being called a lot louder than before. He just set up and looked around and seen a man standing on the other side of the cave. Suddenly the man's figure begins to shine like the sun in the middle of the day. He thought at first this was Gabriel and realized this man was different then Gabriel.

As the man approached him, the light surrounding the man became dimmer and he seen a man that was not white nor Indian but still had brownish skin and had marks on his hands and feet. Gray Fox knew then that this must **YoHeWaH**-Si (Jesus). He fell down to the ground in fear of knowing that this is the Son of the Creator.

He then felt a hand on his shoulder and hearing the man telling him to rise to his feet. Gray Fox stood up with his head bowed in reverence to this holy man. He then heard him say to look up and look at him. Gray Fox slowly raised his head and was quite surprised at how tall this man was.

He then looked into his eyes and seen such compassion and love like he had never seen before in any man he came across in his life. He had dark brown eyes and his hair was down to his shoulders still shinning with a glow. Then **YoHeWaH**-Si (Jesus) spoke to him and told him to sit down and that there were some things he needed to talk to him about. As Gray Fox sat down, he noticed this man hands had round scars on them, and his feet had the same markings.

He then remembered when his mom had told him how the son of the Creator laid down his life for the human race. And how he was tortured by men that drove nails into his hands and feet and hung him on a tree. Gray Fox then asked the man if he could touch the scars on his hands and feet? **YoHeWaH**-Si (Jesus) gave him a big smile and told him go ahead and see and feel the scars that he took for mankind. Gray Fox was astonished how real they looked after all the years that this took place.

Gray Fox told him that now he truly believes that he is the Son of The Creator and that he will do anything he asks of him. **YoHeWaH**-si began to tell the very reason why he was born unto his parents and that he had a great path to walk down and preform great signs and wonders. He told Gray Fox that the Holy Spirit will guide him into all truth and lead him down the pathway of turning his fellow Indians back to their true Creator and to walk in righteousness and holiness before Him.

Also, to let them know that they are part of the Lost Tribes of Israel and He is calling them back unto Him. Gray Fox thought for a minute and said that this task will be hard because of the Evil Spirits that most of them follow and worship. **YoHeWaH**-Si (Jesus) told him that he understands this and that His Spirit will be upon him and will show great signs and wonders through him and that no evil spirit could stand against him; not even Raven the holy man in his camp.

He then warns him that Raven will do all he can to destroy him. But not to fear that He has placed a warrior angel named Michael to protect him until his mission is done on earth. Gray Fox began to ask Him what kind of signs and wonders would he do before his people and other tribes?

YoHeWaH-Si (Jesus) sat there for a moment and then grabbed a burning stick out of the fire and laid it down at Gray Fox's feet. He just stared at the burning stick and wondered why the fire did not burn him? Then he realized that he was a Spirit and not human like him. Then the man told him to pick up the burning stick and throwed back into the fire.

Gray Fox just looked at him and thought there was no way he was going to pick up the burning stick. Then he looked into those brown eyes of compassion and love and knew it would be okay for him to do this. He took a deep breath and picked up the burning stick and threw it back into the fire.

Suddenly the fire grew brighter than ever and then the fire just extinguishes suddenly. Gray Fox was dumb founded in what he just witnessed. Then **YoHeWaH**-si (Jesus) told him to pick up the stick again and throw it down to the ground. So, he picked the stick up and threw it down to the ground and watched the stick become a king snake. This made Gray Fox to jump back from the snake and wonder how this could be?

YoHeWaH-si (Jesus) then told him to pick up the king snake by his tail and hold it in his hand. Gray Fox was first reluctant but decided to pick up the snake by his tail. He bent over and picked up the king snake and it suddenly turned into a rod like what one would walk with in the woods. Gray Fox was then told that he was to take this rod with him where ever his path takes him in life.

And it would be the very tool he needs to show the very power of the Creator against the evil spirits that deceives his fellow Indians. Then he stood up and gave Gray Fox a hug and told him that it was time for him to go and he would always be with him in the Spirit.

Then turned and walked right through the walls of the cave and disappeared out of his sight. Gray Fox wanted to ask him more question, yet he knew what had happened to him this night that change his life forever. He just got on his knees and raised his hands upward and began to praise his Creator for showing him great mercy and grace upon his life.

While he was still praising the Creator, he suddenly felt this warm oil like substance beginning to flow upon his head and down to his feet as before. He heard a small voice telling him to open his mouth and begin to speak the Holy language that his mother knew. Suddenly he opened his mouth an unknown language begins to come forth and he was speaking quite fluently like another language of a different tribe then his. It felt great to him and he started to walk around the cave and began speaking louder and louder in his new holy language.

This lasted over an hour and he could not shake this great feeling he had throughout his whole entire body. Finally, he felt he was done and began to get ready to sleep. So that he can go back to his parent's camp and tell them the great news that he had received his vision and encounter with the Son of the Creator.

Now he knows his mission in life and is ready to face this new adventure. He restarted the fire and went and laid down on his blanket. For he was very tired from this great experience he had tonight of meeting his Messiah and Lord.

Chapter 7

The Night Vision

As Gray Fox got more comfortable in his bedding, the excitement of the evening was making his soul to think about his new calling. He kept telling himself that he needed to sleep and get ready for tomorrow. Finally, he felt himself falling into a deep sleep at last.

It had been only 2 hours since he fell asleep when he thought he heard someone calling his name from a distance. He turned over and shrugged his shoulders when again he heard someone calling his name. But this time the voice got louder and louder and making him sit up in his bed.

Gray Fox looked around the cave and saw no one was in there with him. He scratched his head and thought just maybe he was hearing things in his sleep. Just as he was getting ready to lay down again, suddenly he noticed a fog like cloud was coming into the cave and he could not see anything at all.

He really began to wonder what was going on here in the cave. Then the cloud became so bright as the sun and he cover his head into his bedding. Then heard a voice that sounded much like Gabriel and wonder why the fog like smoke?

Then he seen a man through the cloud standing right in front of him. He knew then that this was not Gabriel but another angel of some sort. As the angel approached him, he told Gray Fox to stand up and it was time to go and see some events that would take place in his life.

Gray Fox stood up and took a step towards the angel when he turned and seen himself still laying down on his bedding. This shocked him and he turned around and asked the angel what is happening to him and what is his name? The angel spoke and told him my name is Raphael and that he was sent to him to show the plans that the Creator has for him. Gray Fox became curious about this spirit realm and he could not wait to share this with his parents. Then Raphael told Gray Fox to come over to the wall where the drawing was. So, he walked over to the wall of the cave and stood there for a moment. Nothing was happening and Gray Fox asked the angel again the purpose of this. Raphael told him to look closer at the wall. So, he did and suddenly the wall disappear right in front of him. Gray Fox rubbed his eyes and thought he was seeing things. He slowly opens his eyes and the wall of the cave was gone. He knew that this was real, and he better pay attention to what he was told to do. He then looked into the open space and saw what seemed like a distant cloud coming his way. He watched it very closely as it made its way to him. He noticed that the cloud was becoming thicker as it approached him.

Before he knew it, the cloud began to surround him and engulf his whole body. Gray Fox could not believe how peaceful it felt being engulfed by this cloud. Then he heard a voice saying to him that what he is about to see are things that will take place in his life as a Prophet unto the Cherokees and the four civilized tribes.

Gray Fox had not recognized the voice and he proceeded to ask who was talking to him? Then he heard this voice say unto him that He is **Y**e**H**eha**W**atte**H**a (I AM your Heavenly Father).

Gray Fox fell instantly to his face and began to worship Him. He could not believe that the very Creator of Heaven and Earth is speaking to him. Then the voice said for him to get up and be prepared to see what in-store for him is. Gray Fox got up and could not see anyone there except Raphael beside him.

Then the voice said for him to pay close attention to what he going to see what is and is to come in his life and the Native Americans in their home land. Then as Gray Fox pondered what was being said to him, the cloud that engulfed him disappeared out of sight.

Suddenly he seen what seemed to be the big pond (Atlantic Ocean) that he had heard that was far East of his camp. He saw the vastness of this body of water that seemed to stretch beyond his comprehension. He was just awe struck of its enormous size and wondered if he would see any land at all. Suddenly he saw many white man's ships coming towards him.

It was like he was seeing an untold number of them coming to his land. Then Raphael came and stood by him and began to explain that over the last hundred years this was the white man from different countries coming to his home land. As Gray Fox kept looking at the untold number of ships coming towards him, it seemed their numbers were getting bigger and bigger. Raphael told Gray Fox that these white men of different countries were really coming to possess and seize the land from the Indians. Just for all the rich minerals and the vastness of the size of this country. This was their Promised Land for wealth and their own land to own.

Gray Fox then turned to Raphael and asked him how long this will last? Then Raphael turned and look at Gray Fox and with sadness in his face. He begins to tell him that these people are from another land. They were filled with much greed and fighting and killing each other for land that was not enough for them. They believe that your land is their new Promised Land for their supposedly religious freedom.

They will continue to come for many generations after your life is over. Gray Fox then paused for a moment and then asked what kind of religion do these people follow?

Raphael began to tell the story how after **YoHeWaH**si (Jesus) death and resurrection in which brought mankind back into the right relationship with their Creator. Then he said about 300 years later a certain country decided to get rid of the lifestyle and beliefs of his people. Which form their own kind of religion that was contrary to your forefather's life and beliefs. It was their holy mission to make everyone to follow their holy teachings and to conquer their land.

Then Raphael looked down to the ground and with a sad face began to tell Gray Fox that this new religion began to slaughter entire country's and every person that stood against them. He then told him that this was a great and dark time for the human race. Gray Fox then asked him why would men do this to each other?

Raphael told him that their hearts and souls were wicked, all because they did not understand the true message of what The Creator had for them when He sent his son to die for them. They perverted the true way of their Messiah and Creator. Gray Fox could not understand why this group of people would kill innocent people who did not accept their religion. Then Raphael told him that this group of people had already tried to convert many Indians with some success. Yet he told him that they will consider you and your people as heathens and savages and ignorant people. Gray Fox asked him what was a heathen? Raphael told him it was a kind of person that did not accept or believe their religion. Gray Fox told him that was silly and could not understand their reason for this.

Then Gray Fox told Raphael that among all the tribes of Indians that was in this region; they all had the same spiritual beliefs and that in no way do they go around killing each other over this. Then he told Raphael that now he understands what the true Spirit is and how it has changed his life. Gray Fox then began to rejoice about his new conversion.

Gray Fox asked Raphael if this religion of the white man had a name to it? The angel responded to him by telling him that in no way do all white man follow this religion that has a dark history to it. He said that many have broken off from this certain religion and trying to walk in the truth of the message of their Creator. R

Raphael told him that this certain group of people call themselves Catholics and other groups have different names for their beliefs. Gray Fox then asked why do they have this odd name for their religion? Raphael told him from the beginning after the Messiah death and resurrection; they call themselves Christian.

Then later after many people left the group of Catholics, they came up with their own names for their beliefs to set them apart from other groups. Gray Fox looked at Raphael with an odd look on his face and asked what does this word Christians means? The angel began to tell him that it is a word that describes people who left their old lives and become born-again through the Messiah like you did. Gray Fox told him that now he understands this word.

Raphael told him to look at the wall and see what was next for him. Gray Fox turned his eyes and looked at the wall that was blank. He turned to see the wall when once again it disappears from his sight. Yet this time he rubs his eyes in disbelief in what he was seeing. He saw the whole country as if through the eyes of an eagle that flies high above the clouds.

Then he looked towards the East and saw where the land met with the Big Pond (Atlantic Ocean) Suddenly he saw what seemed to be a dark cloud coming from the Big Pond. He then noticed a strange looking being sitting on a reddish horse waving a sword that had the name; **"Angelus mortis"** written on it.

Gray Fox did not understand this word and turned and asked the angel what is this word and what does it mean? Raphael told him this was the language of the Catholic leaders and that meant; **The Angel of Death**. Gray Fox turned back toward the wall and saw the angel of death beginning to slaughter an untold number of Indians camps.

This creature even was killing woman and children and babies. Tears began to fall down his face and he turned around not to see this horrific scene that was playing out. Gray Fox did not want to turn around when Raphael told him to and see this horrible scene. He turned around and seen what seemed to be a dark mist flowing through many Indian camps and causing them to have great sores. Then he watched an untold number of them killing themselves because of this dark mist.

Raphael told Gray Fox this was a disease that the white man had brought from their land and carried it with them to their land. For it had killed over 6,000 Cherokees in 2 years. Gray Fox then asked him if this was when he was 4 years old? Raphael nodded his head and said yes and told him that the Creator had protected him and his family from this white man disease.

Gray Fox remembered his mom and dad telling him when he was older about the great disease that almost wiped out the Cherokees and other tribes and even tribes that no longer existed. Raphael told him that in Heaven all the angels and the Creator were very saddened when this took place.

Gray Fox stood there for a moment and watched the scene playout as this dark mist continued to make its deadly path across the entire eastern region of their land. Then he watched as the angel of death caused many Indians to turn on each other all because the white men in Red Coats promised they could stay in their homes if they helped drive out their enemies off their land. Gray Fox decided not to look at the wall anymore and that he had enough of these horrible scenes playouts in front of him. He started to walk away from the wall when Raphael told him that there was one more scene that he needed to see. This was about the future of the Cherokees and other tribes and their destiny for the future.

So Gray Fox turned around and walked back to the wall and stood there unwillingly. He raised his eyes and looked at the wall for something to happen. Suddenly the wall disappears again, and he saw the land again from high above the clouds. Then he noticed that the whole eastern part of their lands was filled with thousands of Indian tribes that occupy this whole region from their earlier days until now.

Raphael told Gray Fox that this was once the picture of all the tribes that lived in this region. For the last 150 years since the white man has landed on this country. The tribes have been driven away from their lands and killed for trying to protect their land. Once he said there were 500 different tribes that was in this region. Gray Fox was astonished of the numbers of Indians in the region and how quickly their numbers dwindled to a small region of land. It was too much for him to comprehend these numbers and Raphael told him in the next 100 years, the population of Indians will drop severely. Then Raphael dropped his head and told Gray Fox that this land of his had as many as 10 million Indians over the last 500 years. Then Gray Fox remembered the paintings on the wall of the Cloud-Eaters (Giants) and the battles that took place in this region.

Raphael told him that he remembers well and that many Indians lost their lives battling the Cloud-Eaters (Giants). Then the picture of this event disappeared from his sight and the wall reappeared in front of him. Gray Fox just stood there and began to try to process all that he had seen this evening.

Then Gray Fox turned to Raphael and told him that he was honored to have him show him these events and that he could not wait to share all this with his parents. Raphael looked him in the face and told him that he was not to share this with anyone at all until later in his life. Raphael told him that before he leaves this place that he will be visited by Gabriel and Michael who will then instruct him further on his mission. Raphael then hugged Gray Fox and told him to be ready for a great and holy mission that he will take in the next few years of his life.

Gray Fox hugged him back and thanked him again for allowing him to witness these events. For now, he understood his purpose in life to bring the Indians back to their Holy Creator and worship Him in spirit and truth. Then the angel told him that his calling and mission will not be easy. That his life will be threatened often. He will be opposing the very evil spirits that are used to having their way with the Indians religious life.

Raphael then turned and walked right through the wall that has revealed the history of Gray Fox's people and other tribes that have been killed and moved out of their land. Gray Fox just stood there for a moment and then fell to his face and began to worship his Creator.

When he was done, he knew that his spiritual journey into his manhood was coming to an end. He got his bedding ready and stoked the fire and was so glad to lay down and get a good night rest. He thought to himself that tomorrow was a new day and his life was going to take the right pathway to reach his people and other tribes for the Glory of his Creator. Finally, he closed his eyes and gave a big sigh and said good night to his new-found Messiah.

Little did he know that outside the cave was a creature like spirit waiting for him to come out so that he can cause deadly harm to Gray Fox. By his side was a hungry black bear who was waiting for his orders to attack his next pray.

Chapter 8

Battlefield Of The Soul

Gray Fox's body was so tired from his Heavenly experience the night before, finally he woke up feeling so refreshed that it this was a brand-new day in his life. He was so ready to go back to camp to share with his parents about his visions. He began to gather his belongings and was ready to step of the cave when Michael appeared at the entrance of the cave. Gray Fox took a step back and began to bow before this angel. Michael told him not to bow and that he was here to protect him the from the danger outside of the cave.

Then Gray Fox asked him what he should do when he got outside? Michael told him when the bear begins to attack you, just take his rod and hit the ground with it. Gray Fox asked him why he could not just use his long stick (rifle). Michael told him the rod will show him the very power of his Creator to protect him. Gray Fox scratched his head in disbelief, yet he told him that he would do what he said.

Michael reassured Gray Fox that he would be right behind him the whole time. So Gray Fox began to walk towards the opening of the cave and looked around to see where the bear was. Little did he know a demon was behind a tree watching his every move. Gray Fox took a few steps into the woods and yet he walked very gently so that he would not make any noise. He kept walking and not knowing this evil spirit was whispering in the black bear ears to attack and kill this young man.

It was like the demon was clawing his crooked fingers into the brain of the black bear. Gray Fox was about 30 yards from the bear when he cried out in a loud roar and started to run towards him. The black bear broke through the heavy bushes as Gray Fox took his stance for battle.

As the black bear made his way towards Gray Fox, he could not believe the bears eyes were black instead of the usual brown. For he could not see the demon sitting on the bears back driving his fingers into his soul. Gray Fox took a deep breath and paused for a minute when he heard Michael's voice telling him in his ear to throw down his rod. So, he put down his long stick and grabbed the rod.

The bear was getting closer when Gray Fox cried out saying," In the name of YoHeWaHsi (Jesus) I command you stop". Then he struck the ground with his rod that was in front of the bear and the ground began to shake violently. This caused him to stumble and fall on his face. The bear lay there for a moment and stood up again to attack his next prey.

Suddenly the bear looked at Gray Fox and saw Michael standing behind the young warrior with a flaming sword in his right hand. The demon looked and saw Michael and instantly jumped off the bears back and vanished out of sight. Then the bear stopped in his tracks and got on all four paws and ran the other direction as fast as he could away from Gray Fox.

Gray Fox stood there for a moment and just got on his knees and raised his hands and began to worship his Messiah. Finally, he got up from his knees to see if Michael was still behind him. As usual he was gone again, and Gray Fox was thankful that he showed up to warn him about the black bear. He picked up the rod and looked at it for a minute and knew that this rod would always be with him no matter where he goes. He got the rest of his things and started to head back home to see his family again. For yet this time everything looked different to him now since he found his Messiah and Creator. It was like he was seeing nature for the way the Great Creator meant it to be seen.

Gray Fox began his journey back to his own camp that was about 5 miles from him. Eventually he came upon his mom prayer hut and saw that it had been torn down. He could not understand why this has happened so he began to run the rest of the way to his home. As he got closer to the camp, he saw Running Bear coming towards him as fast as he could run.

They both hugged each other, and Running Bear began to cry as they both stood there. Gray Fox asked him why he was crying, he had only been gone one moon (month)? Then his friend looks at him with a puzzled look and told him that he had been gone for 4 moons. (months)

Gray Fox told him in no way has it been 4 moons since he left for his spiritual journey. It had only been one moon cycle. Running Bear told him that it had been 4 moons and since he was gone; his parents had been killed by some scalp hunters about 2 moons (month) ago. Gray Fox just stood there for a moment and was in shock in what he had heard his friend just telling him. Gray Fox told him that there was no way he had been gone for 4 moons (month). So, Running Bear told him to come to his parent's hut and see where his mom has been writing down how long he had been gone. As they got into the camp, it seemed the whole camp was watching Gray Fox make his way into his parent's hut.

It felt weird to Gray Fox to see his hut empty of the life of his parents. Running Bear grabbed Gray Fox's hand and took him over to his mother's bedding. He told him to look at the small piece of wood that had scratches of four marks on it. Running Bear told him that each scratch was one moon when he left for his prayer chamber.

Gray Fox just sat there and stared at the piece of wood and tried to figure out how could it be 4 moons since he left the camp! After about 5 minutes of staring at the piece of wood, he turned to Running Bear and asked how his parents died? Running Bear told him that about 2 moons ago that his mom had gone to her prayer hut to pray as usual. Yet this time his Dad went with her to escort her to the sacred place. Gray Fox asked why the 2 normal guards didn't go with her? Spotted Wolf had decided it was okay and even though the two guards protested his decision, they decided to follow them from a distance.

He then said that his parents arrived there, and his mom took her usual position in the hut. While his dad walked around the area for some food. Gray Fox just shook his head and said that his Dad knew better then to leave her by herself like that. Gray Fox hit the floor real hard as if he was disgusted with his Dad decision.

Running Bear began to tell him that as soon as she entered her prayer hut, when the two Indians seen from a distance some scalp-hunters sneaking up to where his mom was. Suddenly they could hear your mom screaming from the hut. That's when your dad came running to her and saw her laying in front of her prayer hut. He tried to pick her up when a shot rang out and your dad fell to the ground. By the time the two guards came upon the scene, they were shocked to see that your father and your mom were dead.

The two began to see where the killer's tracks were leading off to. They also spotted two horse tracks that were leading east of there. Yet they needed to take your parents back to camp for proper burial. Running Bear then told Gray Fox that they noticed that his mom's bracelet was missing from her right arm that he had made for her when he was little.

Gray Fox just sat there in disbelief that his parent was dead. He begins to think how this could happen to him when he was on his spiritual journey to become a mighty warrior. Then Gray Fox gave the loudest war cry he could, his parents were dead and that he was not here to protect them. Then he broke down and started to cry very loud. The whole camp could hear his sorrow, and everyone bowed their heads.

Even Raven the holy man felt sorry for Gray Fox as he stood just outside of his parent's hut. He had to make it look as if he was so sad for Gray Fox's loss. Yet inside of him he just knew this was a great opportunity for him to make Gray Fox the great warrior to finally help to get rid of the white man. Raven figured this situation would give Gray Fox a true motive now that his parents were murdered by white men. As Raven entered the hut, he reached out to Gray Fox and told him that he was sorry for his loss. Gray Fox just ignored him as he wasn't even there. Gray Fox looked at Running Bear with tears in his eyes and asked how come nobody came to find him? Running Bear looked at the ground and told him that they thought you were dead since it had been 4 moons since you left. Gray Fox just put his hand on the ground and started to hit the ground with all his might.

Running Bear just sat there with tears in his eyes and was at a loss for words right now. Gray Fox begin to get angrier and angrier about what had happened to his parents. Yet little did he know that there appeared a big demon just outside his door watching him closely. Its eyes were like that of a lizard and yet not of this world.

Raven closed his eyes with the hope that this demon can finally enter into Gray Fox's body. As he watched Gray Fox getting so angry over the murder of his parents the demon held out his crooked fingers and there appeared a small imp of a demon on his fingers. Then he whispered in the ear of the demon to go and attach itself to Gray Fox's soul. Then the little imp demon attaches his crooked finger into the soul of Gray Fox and made himself comfortable like he was home at last. Just then in the corner hiding behind a blanket and a shield; appear Raphael and Michael the Holy Angels assigned to Gray Fox.

Michael begin to draw his flaming sword to cut the demon into two and send him to the pit of darkness. Raphael stopped him and reminded him that Gray Fox has a free will in this matter unless he chooses to call upon them. Michael told him that he did not like this, but he knew the very Law that the Creator had set when mankind was cast out of the garden.

They both looked on with sadness of what was happening to Gray Fox in his hurt and pain of the loss of his parents. Then they vanished and yet still was watching from a distance when they were ever needed. Gray Fox finally stopped his crying and stood up and looked around the hut and seeing his parents' belongings cried out with a war cry that the whole camp could hear.

Gray Fox turned to Running Bear and told him in the morning he will take some braves with him and hunt down this scalper and will kill them with his own knife. Running Bear could see the hatred that was swelling up in his friends' eyes and told him that he understood.

Then Running Bear told Gray Fox that his father has been made the head Elder of this camp and that he must get permission from him in the morning. Gray Fox put his hand on his friends' shoulder and told him even if his father refuses to let him go and that he was still going anyway, and nobody was going to stop him from getting his revenge for his parents' death. Running Bear then left him alone knowing that this night was going to be hard on his friend.

Gray Fox kept sitting by his mother's bedding and looking at that piece of wood that shows how long he has been gone. He could not understand how this happened to him! Then the thought came to him that maybe he should ask Raphael how this had happened and why was his parents were murdered? Just as he had that thought, Raphael appeared in front of him and reached out to Gray Fox.

Yet Gray Fox took a step back and asked the angel how in the world was he gone for four moons when he knew it had only been one moon? Raphael begin to explain to him that in the Spirit Realm, there is no existence of time as it is the earthly realm. So, in that time the Creator showed you those three events, it had been four moons in your physical realm.

Gray Fox tried to understand Raphael explanation on the time period. Yet for him the issue was why did the Creator let his parents be murdered by white men! Raphael knew what he was thinking and told him that the evil spirits that rule on this earth wanted to destroy his calling by killing his parents. That the Creator allowed this because his parents job was done on this earth.

Raphael with a sad face told Gray Fox he was so sorry for his loss and that he must not let revenge control his soul or it will become a great hindrance in his life. Gray Fox took a step back and told Raphael that he must leave now and that he had many things to think over because this horrible situation in his life. Raphael looked at him and told him that he will always be here for him when needed.

Then he walked right through the hut and was gone from Gray Fox's sight. That night was very long for him because he still can't believe that his parents are gone and now what was he going to do. Meanwhile in Raven's hut, the holy man was rubbing his hands together with some kind of herbs and threw it in the fire. Suddenly the flame grew brighter than ever as Raven began his chant that his holy plans were coming to pass, and his demons were dancing in circles around him.

Raven begin to command the demon that went into Gray Fox's soul to make him angrier and to fill his thoughts with revenge for his parent's death. He began to go into convulsions as he chanted harder and harder to the demon. For he was unaware that the demon was mocking him and knowing that this poor human was his puppet.

As Raven falls and hits the ground, the demons were dancing around their prey and throwing up their crooked fingers and acting like Indians doing a war dance. They were yelling and laughing so hard that even they too fell to the ground.

Meanwhile Gray Fox kept rolling in his bedding and hearing the thoughts of revenge. How could he plan to find those white men and slit their throats and scalp their hair for the grand trophy of his revenge. Then he began to hear a small still voice telling him that this was not right, and it was time to prepare for his mission for the Creator.

Suddenly he cried out and told that voice that he did not want to hear that now. Besides it was his warrior rights to seek revenge for his parent's death. He said then to leave him alone and that it is settled for him to take revenge. Just as he made the comment, Raphael was standing on the other side of the hut and hanging his head in what he just heard Gray Fox comment.

Then he looked towards Heaven and asked the Spirit of the Creator to give him the direction on how he could reach Gray Fox before it's too late. He stood there for a moment and told the Creator thank you for the answer and turned to Gray Fox. He just smiles knowing that in the midst of Gray Fox's anger and sorrow; he will come to his senses in due time.

Gray Fox could not weep anymore and decided it was time to sleep and get the rest he needed for tomorrow. The time of mourning will have to wait till later for him. For he will begin his journey to find and kill those men who took his parents lives. He then spoke softly as if his parents were there and said that he will get his revenge. He swore by his oath and that no matter how long it took, he will get his revenge for their death.

Chapter 9

Revenge

The Sun was just peaking over the mountains with the sound of robins singing of another day and searching for food for their young ones. The women in the camp was getting their fire pits ready to make their families their morning food. In Running Bear's hut, he was going to talk his father about the situation with Gray Fox.

He begins to tell him about the deep anger Gray Fox had about his parent's death. That he wanted revenge and wanted to take a few men with him and hunt down those who killed his parents. His father told his son that Gray Fox had every right to have revenge and seek those who did this to his parents!

He told him that this was his right as the son of Spotted Wolf and Morning Star. He told him to go and tell Gray Fox he had his permission to take four fellow braves with him and bring honor to Gray Fox's family. Running Bear ran over to Gray Fox's hut and found him still asleep. He did not want to wake him but will tell him later after he gets up.

At the same time Raven was getting his ingredients for his next session of chanting before his spirits of bidding. He wanted this time to cause Gray Fox to become so angry that he will forget his mother's spiritual ways. It's just that this was a great opportunity for him to finally reach Gray Fox's spirit and to become the mighty warrior for the Cherokee nation.

As he was getting his things prepared for the holy ceremony; the demon whose name was Destruction was getting ready for Raven to summon him and do his bidding. This was his job that he was a master at. He loved to see people's lives destroyed because of the hatred he had for the human race.

A second demon appeared by Raven whose name was Chaos. It was also getting ready for Raven's bidding to bring all kind of chaos into Gray Fox's young life. The demon then sat upon Raven's shoulder and started to whisper the plan that would bring chaos to Gray Fox. Raven begin to laugh of this plan that he thought he had planned and told this demon to go and start his unholy plans for the young warrior. Raven began to chant harder and harder until his body went into a what seemed to be a trance as he stood by the smoke from the fire. Then both demons screamed out with great joy as they began to go where Gray Fox's hut was. As they approached his hut, suddenly Michael the Arch Angel stood in front of the door and drew out his flaming sword and told them to stop right there or pay the price.

They both stopped and looked at each other and demanded that they have their way with Gray Fox. That his soul and spirit belong to them now. Michael just raised his flaming sword at them. Both screamed that this was not fair and then they vanished out of sight. Michael knew that they would again try to bring chaos and destruction to Gray Fox. He then steps inside of the hut and started to call Gray Fox's name. He had to do these three times before Gray Fox finally woke up. Gray Fox rubbed his eyes and noticed Michael standing by his bedding.

He then spoke to him and told Gabriel that he was not ready to hear what he had to share this morning. Michael looked at him with his piercing eyes and Gray Fox looked down to the ground and told him that he was sorry for his comment to him.

Michael sat down in front of Gray Fox and began to explain to him what the Creators legal rights were on men's affairs on this earth. He told him that the first man (Adam) was given all legal authority over the entire earth and all living creature's on land and water. In other words, Adam was the Elder in charge on this planet's daily affairs. So, when Adam gave into the temptation of the serpent and disobeyed his Creator. He gave his authority over to the Evil One and his kingdom.

The Creator can only interfere when man asks for his help in their lives. Therefore, the Messiah died for mankind to give them legal authority back from the Evil One. It is in His name you have the authority to come against those demons who come against you. Then he asked Gray Fox if he understood now?

Gray Fox looked at him for a moment and nodded yes but then asked why did his parents have to die? Michael told him that their lives were done on earth and it was time for him to take his mother's place and began to reach out to his fellow Indians. For this Message of Righteousness must go out and reach them and bring them back to their Heavenly Creator. Then Michael told him that one day he would see his parents in Heaven when his mission was over with on earth. Gray Fox then told Michael that he now understood but it will be hard for him without his parents love and encouragement. Michael reminded him not to let his revenge get a hold of him because it will bring much chaos and turmoil in his life.

Gray Fox looked down to the ground and told the angel that he will do his best not to let his parent's death drive him to revenge. Michael knew that this was going to be a battle for Gray Fox in the next few days. Then Michael told him goodbye and that he will be here for him when needed for protection from the evil spirits.

Gray Fox watched him walk right through the hut and gave a big sigh and laid down on his bedding and began to ponder these events that has happened to him in the last four moons (months). As he laid there for a about 30 minutes, he started to think about his parent's sudden death and that he was not here to stop it. As he thought about how they died and especially at his mom's prayer hut.

He began to get angry at his dad's
decision of not letting his mom's normal
guards go with them. He started acting
like his father was there and telling him
why he made such a foolish and unwise
decision about telling mom's personal
guards to stay home! Gray Fox became
angrier about his dad's bad decision that
he started to throw things around the hut
and yelling at the top of his voice.

The whole camp could hear the
commotion going on with Gray Fox and
most of them just hung their heads in
sorrow. Raven heard Gray Fox yelling and
began to walk over to the hut to console
him in his mourning of his parent's death.
Raven approached the hut and asked
Gray Fox if he could come in for a
moment?

There was silence for a minute when
Gray Fox told Raven to enter. Raven went
over to him and grabbed and hugged him
like a father. Gray Fox began to weep and
weep like never before in his life. Raven
kept telling him that it was okay and let it
out and that he had the right to be angry
and mourn his parent's death. Raven
begin to explain that his father was like a
son to him that he never had.

And that his mom was a like daughter he never had. After a few minutes had gone by, Gray Fox stopped weeping and tried to compose himself as a mighty warrior of the Cherokee's. Then Raven told the young warrior that the time of mourning was over. It's time to take his rightful place as a warrior and bring honor for his parents' death and get his rightful revenge.

Gray Fox knew he was right and yet he kept thinking about what Michael had said to him earlier. For in his soul it was divided on the action of what was right and what was wrong. Then Raven whispered in Gray Fox's ear as if he was giving a signal to the demon that was in Gray Fox's soul.

The imp of a demon heard the magic words from Raven and began to dig his crooked fingers deeper into the soul of the young warrior. Raven kept speaking to Gray Fox about his rightful duty as a warrior and to bring great honor until his parents. Gray Fox's emotions started to get stirred up with anger over his parent's death and that it was by the hands of the white men.

Then the demon became hysterical by the young warrior's attitude. He began to dig deeper into Gray Fox's soul and started to go into Gray Fox's spirit when he hit an invisible wall. As he tried again to enter, a force of light drove him back. Then he realized that Gray Fox's spirit now belonged to the Great Creator.

So, he stayed in the realm of Gray Fox's soul and made his home. Raven just rubbed his hands as he was greatly pleased by the action of Gray Fox getting outraged by his parents' death. Gray Fox then pushed Raven away from him and told him that it was time to get some warriors together and find the white men and kill them for his parent's honor.

Raven told him that the Chief Elder gave his blessings already to go and find the white men and give them what they deserve. At that time Running Bear came into the hut and said that he wanted to go with Gray Fox and help find those white men! Gray Fox looked at him for a moment and told him that he needed to stay because his time of becoming a warrior was not yet. Running Bear told him that was not fair, and they were best friends in the world.

Gray Fox told him that he needed to stay here and watch his hut. Running Bear told him that it would be his honor to watch his hut and to make sure he brings back the scalps of those white men. They both gave a warrior cry that the whole camp heard. Gray Fox went outside the hut and there were five warriors who volunteered to go on this great hunt for the killers of their former Elder and his wife.

They all raised their bow and arrows and long sticks (muskets) and gave their war cry for all the camp to hear. Meanwhile Raven and his demon cohorts were dancing with great excitement that Raven's prophesy is coming forth. For it had been a long time since they danced all night for a war party.

Finally, they quit for the night and went to get their rest so they could leave early in the morning. Gray Fox knew this is what he must do for his parents and then he will begin his mission for his Creator to reach his fellow Indians. Gray Fox slept like baby that night and was ready for his revenge for his parents. The sun had not risen above the mountain peak when the war party was getting their weapons and supplies ready for their trip. For they didn't know how long this trip would take and really didn't matter to Gray Fox at all. The war party said their goodbyes to their family and Gray Fox gave Running Bear a hug and told him that he will bring back the prize of the white man's scalps to him. They both screamed out as Gray Fox and fellow warriors took off towards his mom's prayer hut where this horrible event took their lives.

As they approached the prayer hut, one of the Indians that had found Gray Fox's parents' bodies; knew where the tracks of the white men and their horses were leading toward the East. Gray Fox stood there for a moment and began to think of all the times he came here with his mother. Especially the time he killed Scarface the black bear that was a great enemy of the Cherokee tribes.

Then one of the Indians pointed towards the East and they all began to follow the tracks of the white man horses. They all picked up their pace as they followed the tracks of the white men. The Cherokees were known for being great trackers in this region.

Gray Fox began to run a little faster cause he felt that they were not far away from them. After going five miles east; they saw a pond which branched off a local river, that was known for a great population of beavers. They figured this is where the white man had to go to do their trapping. They were about half a mile from the pond when they could see the white men sitting in their camp. The war party could see the horses tied up to some small brush that was about 25 yards from their camp.

Two of the Indians made their way towards the horses in a way that the white men did not hear them coming. The other warriors made their way through the tall grass on their stomachs so they would not be seen by the trappers. They were so quiet like a mountain lion getting ready to jump on its next victim. Gray Fox gave the signal that once he shot his arrow at one of the men for the others to charge and overtake them swiftly.

Gray Fox stood up quickly and let out a war cry and shot his arrow into one of the men kneeling by the fire. Chaos broke out as the other Indians made their charge into the camp and hitting the rest of the white men with arrows so that it would not make a lot of noise like the long sticks (rifle) would. It was all over in less than 3 minutes as Gray Fox and others stood over their bodies. Gray Fox noticed one of them was crying for help; when he looked into the white man's face and saw such terror in his eyes. The white man was saying something in French like his father's old friend Francois who also was a fur trader.

Gray Fox then saw his mother's bracelet on his right hand. Anger begin to rise up in him as he grabbed his knife and cut the man's throat and lifted his scalp for the others to see that this was his first kill as a Cherokee warrior. They all gave a loud war cry that Gray Fox had brought honor to his parent's death.

They gathered up the furs and the horses and began their journey back home and to celebrate their vengeance of the white men who killed Gray Fox's parents. It was getting closer to nightfall, so they decided to make camp. They decided not to make a fire knowing that there might be more white men in the area. As Gray Fox made his bedding for the night, he kept thinking about his victim eyes that had such terror in them before he died. He tried to sleep knowing that his revenge has been settled and that he was in the right to take this man's life for his parent's death. He kept hearing this small voice in his soul asking him if this really helped him to get his revenge for their death. He tried to turn over and began to tell his soul to be quiet and get some sleep for the night.

It was a long night for Gray Fox because he kept seeing that man's eyes full of terror when he cut the man's throat. His eyes kept staring at him as if he was asking for mercy for killing his parents. Finally, the sun broke through the morning clouds as the warriors all woke up from their sleep hearing the very sounds of nature. They all were in a great mood because they got revenge for the death of Gray Fox's parents. Except Gray Fox was still troubled by those eyes of the man he killed the day before.

They all had their morning meal of jerky and bread and started their journey back home. They knew it would be late that afternoon when they got back home from their great victory. They decided to take a short cut that would save them around 6 miles of walking. So, they took this other pathway that also led to their camp. About half way home they noticed trees and shrubs had been cut down for some reason. As they walked a little further, they could hear some noises beyond the tree line. They could hear white men talking to each other. So, they laid low among the bushes and saw white men building a fort.

Gray Fox's heart sunk knowing that the white men were this close to their own camp. The warriors backed up slowly and headed back to their camp. They told each other that they must let their Chief Elder know how close the white men were. As they came back into their camp, many of the people were waiting for the good news that Gray Fox got his revenge and his first kill as a warrior.

As they made their way through the camp, Gray Fox went to Running Bear's hut to tell his dad what they saw not far from here. Running Bear grabbed Gray Fox and saw a puzzled look on his face. He asked him if he got his revenge and could not believe Gray Fox's answer. He told him he did but something else happened that he must tell his dad.

Running Bear grabbed him and asked where was his joy of killing his parent's killers? Gray Fox just shrugged his shoulders and told him to leave him alone. Running Bear could not believe what just happened with his friend and the careless attitude about his parents' revenge. Gray Fox then tells his uncle what the war party just saw about 5 miles from their camp. The white men were building a fort and lodges. After talking for a while with his uncle, he turned around and went to his hut and falling on his bedding crying for a reason he could not understand.

Why was this happening to him now? He got his revenge and brought honor to his parent's death. He just sat there and cried some more and thought he just needed some rest after his journey. He thought he would wake up later and all this would be just a bad dream. His parents will wake him up and his life would be back to normal.

Chapter 10

Soul Searching

Gray Fox had been trying to sleep but kept still seeing those eyes of the man he killed. Finally, he sat up in his bedding and began to wonder why he feels bad about taking revenge for his parents' death? He knew that it was his birth right to bring honor to his parents' death but why did he feel such conviction for killing the man.

Then he sat there for a moment and started replaying the scene that was shown to him awhile back about how the white men were going to take over their land and homes. He then realized that vision was coming to pass just like the angel had shown him.

Gray Fox just knew that his tribe and other tribes had to stop them from taking their land and homes. But how would they do this because the Head Chief had signed a peace treaty with the white man. Plus, they had never had problems with them before now. He knew that they would once again break the peace treaty like they have in the past with other tribes. Once again, he became angry over the matter of the white men taking over his land. Just at that time Gabriel showed up standing by Gray Fox causing him to jump out of his bedding. Gabriel told him that he was sorry for scaring him and that he came to give him a message from his Holy Creator.

Gray Fox just looked at him with tears in his eyes and told him that he did not want to talk him right now. Then Gray Fox asked him if he knew that these white men were just five miles away from his camp? Gabriel told him he knew this, and it will get worse for them and other tribes. Gray Fox then asked him why does the Great Creator allow this to happen to him and his people? Gabriel told him that the Creator is allowing this for a greater purpose and this will one day unite the white man and the Indians together to serve their Creator as one people.

Gray Fox told him that this was not fair to his people, but he will try to understand the greater purpose of all this mess. Gabriel told him that he must keep his eyes on his calling as a Prophet unto his fellow natives. That he must not become like other natives who are out for blood, revenge, and great anger to kill all white men they come across. Gray Fox asked what he was supposed to do if a white man came and tried to kill him? Gabriel told him that he must protect himself if needed but his real enemy is evil spirits that will try their best to get him to stray from his holy calling. Gabriel told him that his war is not with flesh and blood but against evil spirts who will try to destroy his soul and spirit for eternity.

Gabriel asked him if he remembered how real the Spirit realm was back in the cave? Gray Fox answered by saying yes, he remembers how real it was and what was shown to him that has happened and what is going to happen in the future for the Cherokee nation.

Then Gray Fox hung his head in disgrace for letting his emotions get the best of him when his parents were killed by the white men. He could not handle the conviction in his soul for killing the man. Gabriel had to remind him that he was only human, and therefore the Spirit of his Messiah must rule and reign in his life. This calling would not be easy for him because his old nature will rebel when walking in obedience to his spirit man.

Gabriel told him that he will be rejected by many of his peers and many of them will try to kill him for betrayal of the Indian traditions. Then the angel told him that as he spends more time with the Spirit of **YoHeWaH**si (Jesus), he will become more stronger in his faith as a Prophet and a servant.

Then Gabriel laid one hand on his shoulder and his right hand on his mouth and began to pray in a language that sounded heavenly. Suddenly his tongue became hot and then as if honey was running down his whole body from the angel's hands upon him. He felt so much peace that it consumed his whole body and tongue that it caused him to fall so gently upon the ground, face first.

Gray Fox laid there for at least 1 hour on his face and worshiping his Creator and Messiah. He felt total forgiveness of taking a man's life through his rage of hatred. He could not believe how he felt and sensing that his whole body felt so clean and pure. He did not want this to pass and wish he could stay in this realm of the spirit and the glory that surrounded his entire body. Finally, he got up on his knees and began to raise his hands upward and started thanking His Messiah for touching his life again and that he vowed to never let anger control his life again. At that time, he felt a cold sensation in his ear coming out and a feeling of warm sensation being replaced in his ear. Little did he know the imp of a demon could not stay in his victim's soul anymore. For the presence of the Almighty had brought a bright light in the realm where the demon had made his home in darkness of Gray Fox's soul.

The demon fell to the ground and began to curse Gray Fox and His Creator while he made his way out of the hut. He turned around one more time to make his attempt to enter Gray Fox's soul when Michael the angel showed up with his flaming sword and pointing to the door of the hut.

The demon tucks his tail between his legs and swore that he will come back again when he sees Gray Fox's weakness in his soul. As quickly as he came before, he vanished out of sight heading back to Raven's hut and for comfort from the other demons. As the little demon made his way back to Raven's hut, the bigger demon looked at him as if he was disgusted that he was no longer in Gray Fox's soul. Then the demon asked him why he was not in his victim's soul anymore? The little demon began to explain how Gray Fox started to worship the Great Creator so much that the Angel Gabriel showed up. The bigger demon asked him why he would be afraid of a Messenger from Heaven?

The demon told him that Michael showed up then with his flaming sword and threatened him to be cut up and sent to outer darkness. The bigger demon told him that this was no excuse for him and the next time to call for reinforcement. Then the little demon began to chuckle a bit and made the comment to his superior that he was no match for Michael.

The bigger demon became so angry that he took the little demon and slammed him down to the ground and began to stomp on him. Raven was totally unaware of these demons fighting each other, while he was making his special potions for Gray Fox. As he was stirring up this special potion, he began to chant to the demons to come and do his bidding. As he got louder and louder, the two demons quit their fighting and looked over at Raven and thought it was time to enter him and have some fun with this mortal man. Suddenly they both jumped into Raven 's body and spirit and started to cause him to go into a wild convulsion. It was a full moon outside when those who are shapeshifters became more impowered by the gravity of the full moon. The demons knew this and thus causing Raven to turn into a black wolf. As Raven finally quit the convulsion, he stood on all fours and made his howling sound to warn the camp that he was here. His eyes were not like any wolf in the natural. They were like a serpent's eyes that seem to glow like they were on fire.

For in each tribe, there was always one person who had the great honor to be a shapeshifter as a certain animal (mostly wolves, owls, and even Mt. Lion's) that they worship. Every Indian knew that the shapeshifter jobs was always to pray on their enemy and to kill or curse their victim.

Then Raven made his way into the woods just behind Gray Fox's hut. As he watched the hut, it was like he could see right through it and see what Gray Fox was doing. He watched as Gray Fox was getting ready to go to bed, and then he came closer to the hut. He began to make his unholy howl as if he was letting his victim know that he was there. Gray Fox could hear the wolf howling and wondered why was this wolf so close to his hut? Yet he was not concerned about the wolf and began to settle into his bedding for the night. He lifted his hands towards the sky and began to thank his Messiah for this day and the protection from the Holy Angels.

As Gray Fox was just falling asleep, he heard this voice telling him to be aware that something was going to happen to him. And that he will be safe, and no harm would come to him. He then turned over and muttered the words of thank you to that voice of the Spirit. He pulled the hide over him and fell into a deep sleep. Just outside of his hut was the black wolf (Raven) walking around in a circle and chanting words of a spell. Raven was asking his spiritual guide to come and help him to cause this spirit take control of Gray Fox's soul and body. As the black wolf (Raven) chanted more and more, suddenly this creature appeared and it stood about 6 foot tall. It had hair like a wild animal that was not of this earthly realm. The stench was like the Sulphur found down deep in caverns below the surface of Earth. This made the black wolf (Raven) bow down before his Master and Lord. Then the black wolf (Raven) stood up on his feet and began his transformation back into his human form. Raven then began telling his Master and Lord that he was at his bidding to do his divine will towards Gray Fox.

Then the huge demon started to chant a certain spell that would call forth this special demon that would possess Gray Fox's soul and body and help him to kill as many white men as possible. After chanting for a minute, this normal size demon appeared and bowed down to his general. This demon had a warrior breastplate that covered his chest. There were smaller demons attaching themselves to his back.

On his breastplate there were certain symbols that was written in a language that Raven did not understand nor comprehend. The taller demon begins explaining to Raven that these symbols on the breastplate stood for certain spells that this demon could conjure up for any special situation.

As Raven looked closer at them, he noticed that there were 12 symbols that had a certain color that stood out from the rest. Raven then asked the warrior demon why 12 symbols? The demon general told Raven that these were 12 special legions under his command. To do his bidding and to place strongholds upon the human race.

Raven was so excited that now he felt that Gray Fox would fall under his spell and become the ultimate warrior for his fellow Indians. He then asked the warrior demon to go and enter the soul of Gray Fox and possess his soul and body. The warrior demon seemed to be preparing his weapon of deceit as he went forth to enter Gray Fox's hut.

As the warrior demon began to enter Gray Fox's hut, he was met suddenly by Michael The Arch Angel that stood between him and Gray Fox. For his flaming sword literally brought a brilliance as bright as the sun. The warrior demon stopped dead in his tracks and fell backwards and stumbled while holding his weapon of deceit. He began to protest to Michael that he had no right to be here in Gray Fox's hut!

Michael started to laugh at the demon and begin to swing his flaming sword at the head of the warrior demon. The demon ducked his head and started screaming that this was not fair and that he will report this to his general. Michael kept laughing at the warrior demon and told him that he better leave while he could or face the ultimate punishment of being sent back into the pit of darkness.

The warrior demon began to shake uncontrollably and started to hiss and curse at the Holy Angel from Heaven. Michael just pointed the flaming sword toward the door and with a commanding voice begin to tell the warrior demon to leave now or pay the cost! Slowly the warrior demon began to make his way back to the door when Michael took his flaming sword and cut off the tail of his so-called opponent and making it scream in great agony.

Just like the demon appeared, it vanished out of sight as Michael put his sword to his side. Gray Fox just turned over and began to sense that he was not alone in his hut. He then raised up out of his bedding and began to ask who was here in his hut?

Michael appeared before Gray Fox and greeted him with a hug. Michael began to explain to him what had just happened here, and that Raven was sending a warrior demon to possess him. Gray Fox told him that he knew that Raven had always had a different ambition for him to become a great warrior and to get rid all the white men in their land. Michael reassured him that he would always be here to protect him from any evil spirits that would do him any harm.

Gray Fox just smiled and thanked him for his protection. They both hugged and Michael turned and walked right through the wall while Gray Fox stood there in amazement of seeing him do this. As Gray Fox got settled again in his bedding, just behind his hut was Raven and the general demon and his warrior was trying to figure how and when they could try to get at Gray Fox again. The general demon told Raven that the Holy Creator must have assigned Michael the Warrior Angel to protect Gray Fox. Raven told the general demon that he had never encountered this holy angel from the Great Creator before. That he did not know that they even existed before now. The general demon told Raven that there has always been warfare between his cohorts and the holy ones from Heaven. The warrior demon spoke up and said that they were the ones that controlled the souls of the human race since mankind was created on earth. Plus, every once awhile there is a human being who truly follows and serves the Great Creator and would ask Him to send forth His Holy Angels to battle for them.

Then the general demon said to Raven that were not many followers of the Creator who knew their rightful place on this earth. For this new religion that mankind is following does not teach or allow them to know their rightful place on this earth. It was all because the very Son of the Creator came and died for them and giving them their rightful authority on earth.

Both demons began to laugh at this religion that has blinded these people into another ritual of bondage that only enslaves their souls from true freedom. Raven told the demons that there must be a way to get to Gray Fox and fulfill his true destiny. The general demon pondered for a minute or two and smiled and said that there must be a way to get to Gray Fox soul and body!

Raven bows down and begins to ask this general demon what are his plans? Then the general demon whispered in the warrior demon ears and he began to dance in a frenzy like manner around Gray Fox's hut. Raven asked why was this demon was doing a war dance? The general demon turned and looked at Raven and told him that this warrior demon was going to have Gray Fox's best friend Running Bear killed by the white men.

Then Gray Fox will want revenge again and thus his soul will be theirs. Raven began to laugh knowing how close the two young warriors were. Then they all began to dance with great joy just knowing this was a sure deal of causing Gray Fox to turn away from his new faith in his Creator. Thus, fulfilling his rightful place as the warrior who will kill all white men.

The general demon took his leave and vanished before Raven. He slowly walked back to his hut for a good night rest. Now he felt confident for the first time in many years that his prophecy will come to pass. Meanwhile in Gray Fox's hut, he just got settled after praying and giving his great Creator all the praise and glory for his new life in Him.

Yet most of all for giving him Michael as his protector in this new walk of life. Now he knows that it is time to bring the message of righteousness to fellow Cherokee's and other Indians of the other 4 tribes. Gray Fox began to fall asleep with the thought that his mom and dad would be proud of him for becoming a mighty warrior for the Great Creator and His Kingdom.

For tomorrow he would start his new journey and start proclaiming a message that he knew would change a person's life forever. Yet he knew that his natives' traditions would be a great stumbling block for his message about the true Creator and His Son that died for their sins.

Chapter 11

The Mission Field

It had been almost a year since Gray Fox's parents have been murdered. He had tried to tell them about the True Creator and his Son who had died for them. Too many of them were entangled in their own religious ways. They rejected his message with great criticism and dismay. Even though they loved him, they began to reject him and his new way of life. There was about 20 or so that accepted his message of righteousness. They were eventually chased out of camp to go somewhere else and make their home.

Gray Fox decided it was time to go out and visit the other camps. He was getting his belongings when Running Bear came into his hut. They both hugged each other and sat down to talk about Gray Fox leaving the camp. Running Bear began to explain to him that he was going to go with him on this new journey. Gray Fox waited until his good friend finished his speech. Then he started to explain to Running Bear that he was too young to go and plus he had not finished his spiritual path to become a warrior. Running Bear stood up and protested that this was not fair, and they were family. Running Bear told him that he needed someone to go with him and that it was too dangerous to go by himself. Gray Fox paused for a moment and told him that he knew that his father would not allow this to happen.

Running Bear said that he did not care what his parents thought. He would not take no for an answer from Gray Fox. As they were talking, Running Bear's father came into the hut to say goodbye to Gray Fox. Running Bear began to tell his father that he must be allowed to go with Gray Fox.

With a very stern face, Running Bear's father told him no again and he must return to his hut. The young warrior let out a war cry and yelling this was not fair at all. Then he stomps out of the hut running as fast as he could out into the woods. Gray Fox felt very sad about what happened with Running Bear. Then his uncle told him that Raven was coming over with this warrior who would go with him on this great journey. Gray Fox began to protest but he kept silent to honor his uncle's wish.

So, his uncle left his hut as Gray Fox
finished his packing, then he heard a voice
at his door. It was Raven asking to come
into the hut. Gray Fox told him to go and
he had nothing to say to him and Raven
stepped inside anyway. Gray Fox stopped
what he was doing and asked him what he
wanted? Raven with a grin on his face told
him that he was going to miss him and
that he wishes that Gray Fox would stay
here with his whole family. He then
reached out his hand in gesture to say
good-bye. Gray Fox decided to be nice to
him and gave him the usual handshake
that was known to the Cherokees.

As they shook hands, Raven began to
tell Gray Fox that he had a surprise for
him and that he will thank him for this.
Gray Fox was wondering what he was up
to and asked him what it was? Then Gray
Fox heard a knock at his door. He is
wondering who this was when Raven told
the person to come on in.

As the stranger walked in the hut, Gray
Fox noticed a very tall and stout warrior.
He had black hair and was wearing a
cougar head and its fur hanging from his
head to his toes. His face was rugged and
a scar running down his right cheek.

Yet his eyes were different than others. They were very dark and piercing like a cougar's eyes. The warrior walks up to Gray Fox and introduced himself as Black Panther. Gray Fox reached out his hand and gave him a warm welcome. Raven begin to tell Gray Fox that this was his apprentice and that one day, he would take over as this camp holy man. Gray Fox asked how come he had not seen him around the camp over the last year or so? Raven begin to explain that Black Panther came from the Paint Clan village. Gray Fox knew that their village was about 2 days journey from here.

Black Panther told Gray Fox that Raven had been coming over and training him for the last five years. Gray Fox with a smile on his face said that he imagines that Raven trained him very well in his work as a holy man! Raven then interrupted him and told Gray Fox that Black Panther was the best hunter and marksman throughout the region.

This was why he wanted Gray Fox to have a companion on his quest. Besides there was a lot danger from the other tribes and most of all the white men. Gray Fox thought to himself that in no way did

Raven care about his safety and most of all his wellbeing. Black Panther looked Gray Fox right in the eye and told him that it was a great honor to meet the very warrior that killed Scarface. Gray Fox thanked him and told him he was just a kid protecting his mom from the old black bear. He then started to tell him about the angel hands on his hands but felt suddenly that he needed not to share this with him. So, they all sat down and smoked their peace pipe for the great journey taking place tomorrow.

Gray Fox felt within his spirit that it would be good to have a companion go with him on this journey. For his father had taught him that it was not good for a lone Indian to go out by himself to hunt or explore. After they were done, Raven and his apprentice left Gray Fox's hut and headed back to Raven's hut. Gray Fox still did not what to think about this new situation. As he knelt down to pray about the matter, he felt a warm wind blowing across his face and head. Suddenly a bright light appeared in front of him and knowing that one of the angels was about to show up. As usual Michael appeared in front of him holding his sword in his hand. They both greeted each other with a hug and sat down for their usual chat. Michael began to explain that he needed to be very careful with Black Panther. For he had been taught very well in the arts of magic and spells. Most of all this young warrior was driven by an evil demon that is very powerful in the spirit realm. Gray Fox said he understood and besides he is has become a man and warrior. Michael had this certain look on his face as not in agreement with what he heard Gray Fox say. Michael told him that he may be able to handle himself with his skills as a hunter and warrior.

But as far as this demon that controls Black Panther, he was no match. Plus, if this demon had his way, he would make sure that Gray Fox would come over to the dark forces. He was not able to fight this demon on his own. Gray Fox shook his head and apologized for his arrogance and knew that he must have Michael's help in these spiritual matters. Then Michael placed his hand on his shoulders and gave him a look as if everything's going to be ok! It was at this time that Michael made his exit as usual. Gray Fox got the rest of his belongings together and was getting ready to settle in for the night. For tomorrow is the big day for he would begin his journey into the mission field. As he lay down on his bed, he was excited but also very apprehensive of this new adventure. Meanwhile over at Ravens hut, the medicine man was finishing his special brew for Black Panther. Then Raven had the young warrior sit down in front of him. It was time to give him the special brew and blow his holy smoke to dedicate him for his journey. Then Raven began to instruct him that it was his job to convince Gray Fox to become the mighty warrior for the Cherokee Nation. That he must convince him that this so-called holy journey will become a disaster for him.

Raven then told Black Panther to use whatever means he could to convince Gray Fox to abandon his holy journey. For he must forsake this calling and become the mighty warrior for his people and all natives. It was time to kill and drive out the white man off their land.

As Raven continued blowing the smoke on his apprentice, suddenly Black Panther was thrown to the ground and his entire body was trembling like someone was shaking him violently. Then suddenly Black Panther's body went limp and he started to raise into the air slowly.

He was about four feet off the ground when he stops. Raven marveled at what he was seeing before his eyes. Then Black Panther began to speak in a deep voice that this human was now under his control. Raven took a step back because he had never seen this before. Then the deep voice told Raven that he will do his bidding and that his mission will not fail. Raven threw himself down to the ground in great fear. As Raven looked at Black Panther's body, he noticed that his body went from laying down to an upright stance without touching the ground.

Then slowly his body stood on the ground and he turned and looked at Raven. His eyes were pitch black and his body had this certain smell like Sulphur and brimstone. Raven's fear became greater then ever at what he saw and smelled from Black Panther's body. Then suddenly his appearance became normal again.

Black Panther stood for a moment like he was in a daze and wondered what just happened to him. Raven began to ask him if he remembers anything at all? The young warrior told him all he could remember last was when Raven blew smoke over his entire body. It was getting late and they both bedded down for the night. Finally, the sun was peeking behind the clouds and spring was in the air. Today is the big day for Gray Fox and the excitement was building within his soul and spirit. This was his very first time in his life of leaving the valley he called home. As both warriors started to walk away from the camp, Gray Fox could hear Running Bear yelling from the ridge. He turns to see his best friend standing and raising his voice like a mighty warrior. The whole camp was watching as the two warriors made their way through the valley.

For the next three days, they made their way into the Southern part of the Tennessee Valley. Finally, they came to the camp where Morning Dove grew up. As they drew closer to the camp, they are greeted by a war party. They were taken straight to the Chief Elders hut. As they were approaching the hut, a tall slender old man came out to greet them.

Gray Fox greeted the Chief Elder with the usual handshake and began to tell him that he was son of Spotted Wolf and Morning Dove. The Chief Elder grabbed him and gave him a great big hug. It was a great honor to have his niece's son here at his camp. The old man told Gray Fox that he had heard what had happened to his parents. With tears in his eyes, he told Gray Fox that he was glad that he did not get killed with them. Gray Fox asked him if he had heard that he killed his parents' murderers? The old man nodded his head and thought it brought honor to his family's legacy. Then Gray Fox introduced Black Panther to the Elder and that he was from the Paint Clan. The old man gave him a warm hug and told him that his home is their home anytime.

The Chief Elder welcomed them both to come and sit down and have supper with him and his family. For the next 3 hours, they ate and talked about Gray Foxes parents and how his mom was such a special woman growing up in their camp. And that Spotted Wolf was like a younger brother to him that he never had before. As they got settled for the night, the Chief Elder told them both that tomorrow they would have a great festival in their honor. Both young men told him that they were honored to be here and for letting them stay in the guest hut. They all gave each other hugs and made their way to the guest hut. As they both began to settle down for the night, Black Panther excused himself from the hut to get some fresh air. As he left the hut, Gray Fox got on his knees to start his ritual routine of praying to his Great Creator. He then raises his hands high into the air and began to worship with his spirit language. Suddenly he could smell a sweet aroma in the hut. Suddenly Michael the Warrior Angel appeared in front of him. He greeted Gray Fox with his usual salutation and they both hugged each other.

Gray Fox began to ask him why he was here when Michael told him to be quiet for right now. Michael began to tell him that he was in grave danger and to watch his back concerning Black Panther. For there is a very powerful demon spirit that is controlling him. There will be a great battle soon and that the Great Creator had plans for Black Panthers life. Gray Fox asked what he meant about this? Michael just told him to watch and see Black Panther be set free from this demon that controls his spirit and soul. Then his sword became like fire and Michael reassured him that he will take care of that demon for good. Gray Fox marveled at the flaming sword and told Michael that he would not want to be on the end of that sword when he uses it. Michael told Gray Fox to start praying for Black Panther's soul that he would come out of that dark realm and enter the very Kingdom of the Great Creator. Gray Fox told him that it would be an honor to pray for him and to see those demons off his friend. Michael grabbed Gray Fox and told him not to fear of what is getting ready to happen to him and his friend.

Gray Fox heard Black Panther at the entrance of the hut. Suddenly Michael vanished as the young man entered the hut. They both said good-night and got into their bedding as they could hear wolves off in the distance from them. Black Panther just smiled knowing that it was almost time for his host to take over him. Gray Fox very quietly began to pray in his spirit and soon fell asleep for the night.

Just outside their hut, there was a group of demons watching the hut from the trees. They were anxious for the word to go and cause great havoc among the Indians. While on the other side of the hut, stood seven warrior angels with Michael waiting for the demons to make their move. The whole camp was silent except for the night creatures making their ritual night calls. The stars in the Heavens were brilliant during this time of the year. Little did anyone know that a great battle would take place tomorrow within their own camp. A spiritual battle that would determine the very outcome of a young man who was called to be a Prophet to the Five Civilized Tribes and their destiny in the white man world.

For the first time in hundreds of years, the holy angels were ready and prepared to battle their arch enemy's. It was up to them to make sure this young prophet would stay on the right course for the Kingdom of Righteousness and the Holy Message. To bring back the Natives of this new promised land back into the true ways of their ancient fathers in Israel.

The Heavenly Angels knew the stakes were high in this battle. Yet they were confident they would win this battle for Gray Fox and his people. Then Michael told Gabriel to go and give Gray Fox a dream of what is getting ready to happen in the spirit realm. Gabriel got his orders and started to enter the hut where the two men were sound asleep.

As he got closer to the door, all of a sudden, he was thrown back about 50 yards from the hut. He was surprise of what just had happed to him. He pick himself up and turned to looked and saw it was one of Azazel princes that had attacked him. The battle for Gray Foxes soul and spirit had just begun just before the sun came up. **THE BATTLE WAS ON!**

Don't worry his story will continue in the sequel book called: The Unknown Prophet: The Great Exodus in 2019

Made in the USA
Columbia, SC
18 May 2019